£2.50

For Joan,

with very best wishes,

Bridget

At Miss Mulligan's and Other Stories

Bridget O'Toole

The
Drumkeen
Press

At Miss Mullingan's
First Published July 2009
by
The Drumkeen Press,
35 Springtown Road,
Derry, BT48 OLT,
Northern Ireland.
Email: thedrumkeenpress@hotmail.co.uk

ISBN: 978-0-9553552-1-9

The moral right of the author has been asserted

Produced by Beta Printing Services

For Molly and Brendan

Bridget O'Toole grew up in Cornwall, taught for many years at the University of Ulster and now lives in Donegal. Her late husband was the environmentalist, Barney Walsh; their two children, Molly and Brendan, are now grown up. Her stories have appeared in *The Honest Ulsterman, The Sunday Tribune* (where she was shortlisted for a Hennessy Award) and *Fingerpost's* Christmas Anthology. She also contributed to the *Phoenix* and *Faber* anthologies of Irish Short Stories.

CONTENTS

ACKNOWLEDGEMENTS

Acknowledgements are due to the editors of the following publications in which some of these stories first appeared: *The Faber Book of Best Irish Short Stories* 2006-7, *Phoenix Irish Short Stories 2000, The Honest Ulsterman, The Sunday Tribune, North West Christmas Anthology.*

Special thanks to editor, David Marcus, for his kindness and critical encouragement.

Thanks to Dolores Meenan for her unfailing help and support.

ON A HOT DAY

Maria sat in the passenger seat of a rented car. It was a hot day. 'He's driving too fast,' she said to herself, 'he's trying to get away from *us*.'

She was tense. This was partly because of their speed; it was a narrow country road. But she had been tense for days now, all during their visit to her home.

He braked suddenly. A few cars were in front of them, moving slowly. 'Cattle,' she said. He replied, 'No. Human beings.'

They came up to people walking on both sides of the road who seemed to be calling to each other in chorus. Through the open window she recognised the rise and fall of voices − it was the Hail Mary − and saw rosary beads. They were women mainly, wearing bright summer clothes, and young girls all walking purposefully. Not all were praying, some were laughing and two girls had flattened themselves against the hedge grinning in exaggerated alarm at the traffic. The rest kept to the road so that the cars had to move slowly.

'Oh my God', growled Maria once they had left them behind, 'That's another reason I could never live in this country.'

Antony, who was now driving more moderately, asked, 'Where d'you think they were going?'

'It must be the open-air Mass.'

Very soon they came to a field whose gate was open; a few people were gathering near the back of a lorry. On this was a table with a white cloth, flapping gently in the breeze, held down by candlesticks.

'How fascinating,' said Antony, 'Like the days of the Mass rocks. Does it happen every year?'

'No, it must be some kind of anniversary.'

Antony's enthusiasm for her native land had led Maria to feel an alienation both from Ireland and from him. All that was most naïve and pale and vulnerable about him seemed to come to the fore when he admired her father's stone walls or traced the inscriptions on an ancient cross. He was simply puzzled at her irritation.

Now they were going to look at a house further along the road. Perhaps because he sensed he was losing her Antony had already brought her to several properties in which she might be confined. There was a tall, narrow terraced house in Moville overlooking Lough Foyle and a modern bungalow with arches and large windows showing a view of the mountains. In each case the estate agent had been with them. Today it was just the two of them and they had the key.

The place was less than half a mile further on. They knew the house at once from the estate agent's picture. It was small and rather graceful but faded looking. The white paint of the walls had become a little dull and patchy and the blue paint round the windows was peeling. On the front path a rhododendron almost blocked their way, its base lost in tall stinging nettles.

'I don't know why we're doing this,' Maria thought, as Antony unlocked the door.

Inside, the house was hot and dark. It smelled of fungi and dying vegetation as though it were buried in a deep forest. They drifted in separate directions. Maria's high-heeled sandals echoed in the quiet. She found herself in a room with one small window. It scarcely lit the room, which was full of palpable shadows. But the window itself showed a bright world – shining green leaves and red fuchsia branches perfectly framed in the surrounding darkness. It was so intense that she stared and then looked away until the shadows in the room faded and she could see that it was empty. Only a fireplace remained, a pretty one with a curved grate. The tiles surrounding it were

3

green and had not lost their shine although soot had fallen into the grate along with twigs from some nest-building.

Attracted to the fireplace she turned away. It had too much charm; it could lead to unwise decisions and then not have the weight to support them. No they could never marry. His goodness made her bad. This little room was like the 'good' room at home and she saw herself as a hunched spiteful fairy the way she had sat there with him and her parents and could not even smile at him. They had been sitting in the evening light after tea. Her father was relaxed with the Englishman now, telling him all kinds of tedious stuff about sheep and ditches and stray dogs. It was a relief when the men went out and she heard their voices in the yard, Antony's with his polite questions, her father's confident rumble. The women sat in the tidy, awkward room where recent dusting had released shafts of dancing light. Maria closed her eyes and willed her mother to go on not saying anything. She felt she regressed whenever she went home, a twenty-five-year old behaving like a teenager, sullen, edgy, trying to control even what she was rejecting. Even her mother's spice jars enraged her. She put her nose to stale nutmeg and cinnamon. 'Don't you ever throw anything out?'

'Not if it's still good.'

*   *   *

4

Returning to house-viewing she met Antony at the top of the stairs. She would not let him speak but smiled politely before turning away as though they were visitors to a stately home. But a few minutes later, his call could not be ignored.

'Maria, do come! Look!'

He was looking out at the back garden. 'Look a fuchsia hedge!'

It ran down one side of the garden. It was in magnificent flower, guarding a jungle of nettles and dandelions.

'Imagine,' he said, 'growing potatoes in the shelter of that!'

'The complete Irish picture,' she thought.

'It wouldn't prevent the blight,' she said, but gently.

Now she found his enthusiasm so insane as to be almost endearing. He looked resolute, as though any minute he would tackle the nettles and long grasses. His joy surprised her, the way it survived her days of sullenness. She returned to the other upstairs room. There was a view of Slieve Snacht with all the brightly coloured fields running up the side of it. In proportion this little house fitted the scene well.

The room had a window in the gable wall. From it Maria saw the field where the open-air Mass was taking place. She heard nothing, just saw the crowd standing there in their bright colours. She wondered if Antony had looked out at it too.

'I am just a tourist,' she told herself, 'on an unconducted tour.'

Down in the kitchen she found a large deep sink with a blue-ish green trail where water had been. She rested her bare arms on the side of it, feeling the coolness. But when she tried the single tap, there was no water. Suddenly Antony was behind her.

'Pity,' he said, 'I'm terribly thirsty.'

They unlocked the back door and went out together.

'Your fuchsia hedge blocks out the mountain,' she remarked.

'I don't care. I love it!'

Near the bottom of the garden they met a curtain of midges.

'Does the garden go on?'

They passed through a gap into a further patch with a small hillock in the middle of it. It was wilder here with gorse and brambles. In the hot sun the smell of gorse filled the air. What did it remind her of, Maria could never decide. Was it peaches or coconut? The ground sloped down towards the hillock which was covered in gorse, its richly clustered petals full of bees. At their feet, hidden in the long grass, a few white-painted stones suggested a path. They followed it, and on the far side of the mound discovered a door.

'Ah!' Maria's gasp was of pleasure and recognition.

Now she could show him something.

The door was not fastened, only propped. Maria moved it to one side pushing against bracken, 'Look!'

It was the well. They peered into the darkness. Moving the door had dislodged a yellow blossom which was now floating on the surface of dark water. Three steps led down to it and there were more below, leading out of sight. All at once, Maria was joyful. 'Come close,' she said and taking off her sandals, stepped down, then crouched and cupping her hands, scooped up water.

'Go on, drink it!'

He giggled slightly and drank from her hands. 'Oh it's lovely!'

'Have more.'

'You have some!'

They were laughing and gasping but all the time taking and drinking the water carefully. Then they sat on the grass side-by-side and Maria started to tell him about the well at her grandparents' place.

'It was very like this with a door and steps down. One day, a hot day like this I had to get in and clean it out.'

'Oh! How do you clean a well?'

'I'd to put on my swimming costume and take a bucket and shovel and just clean it. We'd had a drouth so it was lower than this but I remember being frightened because they said "Stop when you get to the bottom step" but I didn't know which was the bottom step and I was reaching down with my feet into – maybe nothing. The main thing was it was very, very cold. And my swimming costume was getting too small for me and a few people came to watch and I was embarrassed.'

'Poor Maria! I hope they went away again quickly.'

'They must've. Anyway I had the water fairly churned up by the time I'd finished.

'After I came out, everyone made a fuss of me and I sat by the range wrapped in a blanket and drank tea while the grown-ups had theirs and finally my teeth stopped chattering. They all went outside again and left just me and my Granny and it was peaceful there with just the chink of the cups and water rinsing. Everything looked so beautiful, the bit of yard you could see through the open door, chairs and the table with just one plate left on it, it was all perfect. It was as though cleaning the well I had somehow – transformed everything.'

She wanted to stay in that memory. It wasn't necessary to say, 'Of course it didn't last.' And sensing that it should stay intact, he said nothing. Another time he might ask her, 'And did the water taste better afterwards?' but he just sat beside her near the well, listening. There was the murmur of insects and a car going by in the road.

They walked back to the house. Her dress was sticking to her front where she had spilt water. She could talk again now. 'This place does remind me of my Granny's only it's more elegant somehow.' She started chattering about all kinds of things then – how when she made her first communion her Granny had been sick and she had to go and visit her all dolled up in her white dress and veil and tell her everything. And how if the cousins were there they would all be jealous and fight.

As she spoke they both realised that her wish not to think positively about home and Ireland had stifled the communication between them. Now at last the heaviness was slipping away.

But as they walked through the house he became very quiet. There was no capping of her reminiscences with tales of his own childhood. At the gate he stopped. 'I'm glad you talked to me again. It somehow makes everything clearer.'

'Oh is that good?' She thought his manner seemed very serious.

'Well I think I see things clearly, how things are.'

'Is that good?' she asked again.

'It's not Ireland you don't want, or the Catholic Church, or the tourist industry or any of that stuff, it's me. It's me you don't want.'

For the last ten minutes she had been absorbed in stories and memories. She hadn't thought about him at all, or them.

She had no idea what to say. It was clear from his tone that he was making a statement, not asking a question.

They walked slowly to the car. 'I'm sorry Maria, I don't want you to be unhappy. It's just that I see now I've been deluding myself.'

'And to think,' she said to herself, 'at the well we seemed to be blessed.'

She was frightened to reassure him so she said nothing and they sat in the hot car in silence. She pressed the palms of her hands into her thighs to dry the sweat. 'Nice little house,' he said too lightly and started the engine.

They heard singing as they passed the open-air Mass. Maria recognised the tune but could not hear or remember the words. He drove quite slowly. She looked in the wing mirror and saw their retreat unfold before her, the narrow road, the green hedges and sometimes a brilliant bush of fuchsia which filled the whole frame.

INFLUENCE

Has anyone ever explored the relationship between the un-washed saucepan and the un-written poem? In the life of the single person writing at the kitchen table the dishes may be emblematic. Are they unwashed because the creative impulse has pushed them aside? Or are they soaking while the writer's mind saturates in words and images waiting to catch the moment?

I never associated Alice with dirty dishes. But then I never connected her with writing either. It was a surprise when she started to publish novels. I was indignant – she wasn't supposed to be the writer – I was. Even when her titles appeared on the best-seller lists I didn't quite believe it, or perhaps I thought I would 'catch up'. I had taken sabbatical leave from teaching in a department which encouraged creative writing and the leave was specifically granted to work on a novel. I was busy 'germinating ideas' on a beach in France when I saw *Breezes from Heaven* by Alice Clarkson lying face-down on the sand.

The sun would warp it. Shock and envy were there but also I thought it a shame that anyone should treat her book in such a way, abandoned next to the Ambre Solaire with its spine cracking. Alice would have hated it. She was tidy and had a muted respect for objects.

We first met in our teens and in those days her appearance might have misled you. She looked feather-headed – physically. Her hair was soft and fluffy and always seemed to be lifted by a breeze and haloed by the sunlight of that distant time. We used to go sailing together. She always wore makeup. Blinking and peering into the glittering path of the sun, her eyes would water and by evening the smudgy eyes and tousled feathers made her look vulnerable and slightly dotty. Her calm manner contradicted this, she was poised and self-sufficient. Men clustered at the water's edge to help us ashore. It was always Alice who made sure the dinghy was exactly centred on its trailer. Later, in the boatyard she was quick and accurate in making up the sails and fastening the cover smoothly and neatly. She seemed to be able to work and talk at the same time. I meanwhile, with short straight hair and the kind of looks which brought no-one running to the shore, would have my fingers stilled by an anecdote and would stare mesmerised at the thistledown drifting past the dark rocks. Its shining delicacy had me in a dream but then I would try to find the exact words to catch it. Standing in a trance with a length of line in my hand while Alice did the work I scarcely needed to justify – I was going to be a writer.

Alice didn't savour words particularly, she just used them to communicate. I thought it odd when she started to write fiction.

During the sabbatical I was having trouble producing anything. The ploys to keep pen from paper became more and more sophisticated. I took to roaming the bars of the town, doing 'research', widening the range of my material, even for a few early evenings taking my paper and pen with me to sit in a quiet corner where the varnished table and bright glasses became for me a 'clean well-lighted place'. One evening I ran into some of my tutorial group and their jokes and insults made me realise how much I missed them. I invited them to a dinner-party. Since I never cooked it was necessary to spend the whole of the next day studying cookery books and buying food.

I passed a morning happily admiring, coveting even, Elizabeth David's prose style while the afternoon required a walk to 'Gerard's Garden' where you could buy fresh herbs. My *paupiettes de boeuf* demanded no less. The day of the dinner was taken up with cooking and the evening was all drink and gossip, and, after they had gone I sensed my loneliness once more.

The next day, with a slight hangover and surrounded by unwashed casseroles, I made myself sit down and write an account of the evening. This was discipline. It was also pointless. Was it any more valuable or permanent than the discarded wooden toothpicks which had held the stuffed beef together?

For years Alice and I had exchanged only Christmas cards. If I'd felt close I might have read one of her novels out of friendship. But envy made a barrier and there was also my fear of being influenced by other styles. So Alice remained closed, just in case, along with Virginia Woolf and Muriel Spark. Instead I read the stories of Chekov and became paralysed entirely.

When Alice suddenly wrote to me I forgot for a moment about her fame. She and Alastair, her husband, wondered if I would be free to join them and a friend, Martin, on a sailing trip. And before that, might Alice visit me for a few days while Alastair was at a conference in my university?

I was amazed and suspicious. Who was this friend Martin? Were they matchmaking? Surely she must realise I'd forgotten everything about sailing. The worst thought was that she might be coming to stay in order to make sure that our friendship still had enough substance.

All these suspicions were real but the prospect also filled me with hope. My flat was becoming a prison with its crumpled pages and lifeless typewriter. Best of all, and I never really let it surface, was the possibility of being wanted. Being a writer can make you feel very low about yourself.

I invited Alice to stay, of course. Now I would have to read one of her books. They weren't hard to find. *Penelope's Picnic* was at the supermarket check-out. Too many years teaching literature had not only strangled my capacity to write, they had also distorted my reading. As I might have expected, *Penelope's Picnic* was well organised, well structured. The characters were morally undemanding. Then I began to realise that her not being interested in words was an advantage. Yes, she did just use them for communication. No ambiguities, no tormented pursuits of the exact phrase, no seductive verbal distractions prevented her from getting on with the real job – telling the story. It was all very clear-sighted and I became absorbed. Perhaps the characters were rather shallow. But Alice wasn't patronising them. The book had warmth and niceness and it soon stopped being a chore to complete before her visit, it turned into a reminder of Alice herself. I looked forward to seeing her – I could write that sentence now without reservation.

I was a little worried about how we would pass our time. Much could be achieved and lost in four days. Would we write away at our books? Drink and talk late into the night? I even felt nervous and tried to decide if this was because of her success. At her estimated time of arrival, she arrived. She still wore make-up but it was very understated. Her hair was shorter, still cut in layers but sleeker. Now I realised my shyness had to do with her self-containment and this had always been there. Her being so matter-of-fact made me think I would talk too much, feel too much and get things wrong. Her poise was not unfriendly.

'Let's go out,' I said, 'I know a good pizza place.'

'Couldn't we stay in? We'd be together more.'

She showed me how to make a white sauce, amazed at my lack of equipment.

'Don't you have a wooden spoon? How do you manage?' She explained that you can't rush the making of sauce. 'I find it peaceful somehow, it's soothing'. She stood there, talking to me and yet, with a concentration that was like love she stirred gently, flinching only slightly as the metal spoon scraped the metal side of the pan. I wanted to ask her all kinds of things. 'Is your life in need of peace?' 'What's it really like to be married?' I had also been wondering whether it was fate or choice that prevented them from having children. Fate or choice... The sort of verbal pairing which could doom me to endless, fruitless meanderings...

'What are you thinking of?' she asked and then more formally, 'You must let me tell you about Martin.'

The truth was I was scared of meeting strangers so I had simply put him out of my mind.

'We met him at the sailing club. He's nice. A bit younger than us. Full of ideas. I mean your sort of ideas. I think you'll enjoy talking to him.'

I made awkward interested noises and hoped the subject would go away.

Alice stirred cheese into the sauce and we ate it with pasta and hard boiled eggs.

'There's a much quicker version,' said Alice, 'where you boil eggs and open a tin of macaroni cheese. Useful for sailing or camping. We're not matchmaking with you and Martin. And – you know – you're not sharing a cabin or anything.'

It was clearly time to show some enthusiasm. 'It'll be fun to meet someone else, I mean not colleagues or students, someone else to talk to.'

We didn't stay up late drinking and exchanging confidences. I asked if she would be wanting to write the next day.

'Good Lord, no! I'm on holiday.'

Because I couldn't ask the profound questions I needed to, I asked about something which interested me just as much.

'What sort of a routine do you have?'

'Routine?'

'You know, do you write at night, in the mornings, when?'

'Oh, I see. Well, after I've washed the breakfast things, I hoover around a bit if it needs doing and then go into the study and get down to it.'

'Then? Till?'

'I don't bother with coffee till lunch-time. I have some then with bread and cheese. Then I go for a walk and I'm back at the desk by three and I write till Alastair gets home sometime after five.'

'You don't actually write all the time do you? I mean surely sometimes you do your nails, or go to the Post Office.'

She laughed. 'Not when I'm writing.'

'Do you actually, you know, *enjoy* writing?'

'Yes,' she sounded surprised at the question. 'Why? Don't you?'

'When it comes I do, but sometimes it's agony, just getting the words out.' I showed her on an index card the judgement of Dr Johnson on the subject of Thomas Gray, that "he had a notion not very peculiar, that he could not write but at certain times or at happy moments, a fantastic foppery, to which my kindness for a man of learning and virtue wishes him to have been superior."

Alice was more sympathetic. 'Why do it then, Sal? You have your job and you like that. You don't have to write.'

'If I knew the answer to that, I might be able to finish my novel!'

I put away my papers and began to enjoy Alice's holiday. I liked seeing her vanity as she rearranged bookstands outside shops to display her titles to advantage. On the last evening we tidied the flat; we would leave together the next morning. She washed the dishes while I decided what book to take, knowing that sailing could mean long afternoons listening to the rain on the cabin roof.

'Don't bother about bringing anything. Alastair has all Patrick O'Brian on board.'

Then she asked,

'I'll throw the dishcloth away shall I?'

'Whatever for?'

'I used to find, coming home after the holidays that the whole place would smell slightly of something which turned out to be the old dishcloth, no matter how clean it was.'

'Yes, OK. Go ahead.' and it went with empty yoghurt cartons and coffee grounds into the plastic bag which was tied neatly and left in the dustbin the next morning.

*   *   *

Alastair was now very bald and seemed at first to be obsessed with academic matters. No sooner had we hugged − 'Sally, it must be years' − than he told me in dramatic detail of a dispute which he had won, with a Dutch Professor of Physics. But, like Alice, he could put work behind him.

By the time we reached the coast he was singing arias from Puccini. That was how they had met, I remembered, singing in a choir.

I was completely at ease with Alice again. I thought that of all the practical things about her I would probably always remember the hint about the dishcloth. I had read too much, lived too much in the head and yet certain indissoluble material facts about people have fastened them in my mind. I think of an aunt, making lemon pudding, wincing, holding her hands like claws and saying, 'Have you noticed how lemon juice will search out any little cuts you have?' A teacher of philosophy with a passion for theological debate is kneeling at her fireplace, her face glows, not from the fire, which has yet to be lit, but with a zeal to uncover ideas, and yet the thing I most remember is the way she folded and then twisted newspaper into tight knots for starting a fire. Every time I light a fire I fold the newspaper into narrow sticks before twisting and tying them the way she had shown me, and every time, if only for a moment, I think of her. Now Alice had guaranteed that even if I forgot our youth and never read another of her novels, I would think of her whenever I left home for more than a few days.

He was waiting on the quay with a wedge of sunlight on the water behind him so that I could tell nothing except that his hair was curly, he was slim and perhaps a little tense. When we were closer I could only glance quickly at him because he was embarrassingly good-looking. I took in brown hair, green eyes with dark lashes, even a few freckles. I had not expected this because he'd been characterised to me as a sort of soul-mate.

He was attractive but obviously twenty years younger. This might not have mattered if he had not himself acknowledged it in his manner to me. He was gentle, almost deferential. Straightaway he referred to some reviews I'd done for *The New Provincial*. I was unable to be gracious.

'Oh God, did you read those? I thought the whole point of *The New Provincial* was that nobody read it.'

This sullen response he treated as though it were the frothiest wit. He was nice, I could tell that, and once I'd got used to him, a pleasure to look at. But he was also relentlessly intellectual. I went round the boat trying to remind myself of the gear. Which of these lines thickly clustered round the mast

21

was the main halyard, which the jib and what was this other one for? As I tried to keep my feet and squinted upwards Martin appeared at my elbow. 'What you were saying in the Arthur Symons review about urban poetry, I wondered, did you ever read... there's a fascinating footnote of Walter Benjamin's piece on Baudelaire...' It was all Benjamin and Adorno and I admired them both but what I probably needed was a copy of *Swallows and Amazons*. I told him this and he had just read Arthur Ransome's autobiography and wanted to talk about Ransome's account of democratic centralism in action. I liked him best when I was sitting up on the foredeck and he was down in the cockpit helping Alastair and I could just look at him without having to talk.

We had soft winds and sunshine. I began to drift into a dream world, a drowsy retreat from consciousness with a slight, pleasing heaviness which was with me all day. It was more a retreat from thinking, because physically I was well awake. I stopped thinking about my novel. Lying on my stomach in the bows I could feel every rise and thud of the boat against the water, hear the tearing of the bow-wave, smell it even, and sometimes get a dash of spray on my arm. Sometimes I would just gaze, sit beside Alice in the cockpit and stare out at the long stretches of water between us and the shore.

'Do you remember when we came here one day,' asked

Alice, 'and it looked as though there was a lake on the headland flowing down to the rocks?'

'Yes. I do remember. It was bluebells.'

'They were so thick.'

'And just the same colour as the sea.'

'Like a mirage.'

Martin said, 'It sounds like magic.'

I could see why Alice and Alastair were so fond of him. I liked him too. He seemed free of ego problems and was truly interested in other people. Later he asked about my novel. 'It's buried,' I said, 'full fathom five. Drowned the characters. Sent their world into outer space.' Then thinking I'd been rude, 'Do you write fiction?'

'No, not really. I write poetry.'

'Oh.'

'But hardly any published.'

'Well, maybe...'

'Come on, it's time to go ashore.'

One day it was cloudy and sluggish. The water seemed to be all surface, grey with a sullen shine. I trailed a line for mackerel, so did Martin. Alastair was between us, steering. It was Martin's first time fishing.

'How will I know when I've got one?'

'You'll just feel it.'

The line was cutting into my fingers. I would change its position in my hand and pull it forward sometimes, partly to remind myself of the weight of the lead. Sometimes the bite is sudden and unmistakeable, at others it just feels like an added heaviness and even when you pull it in you can't be sure until the fish is on the surface.

Martin was first. 'I think I've got one!'

Alastair tested his line. 'Yes, feels good.'

As he brought the fish in, Martin cried 'It's beautiful', and it was certainly the brightest thing on that cloudy morning, shimmering green and purple and pink as it skidded from side to side.

'What do I do now?'

'Give it to Sally,' said Alice, 'she'll break its neck.'

I caught its flickering body, held it firm and took out the hook. Then I put my thumb in its mouth, feeling the row of tiny teeth against my skin, bent its head right back till the neck was broken. The fish went into a bucket where it twitched a little. I couldn't see Martin's face but Alice said, 'It has to be done. You wouldn't want it flopping around gasping for water, would you?'

'No, no of course not,' but for a while he didn't look at me. I wondered if this is the thing he'd remember about me when all the words had gone.

We caught six fish and Martin offered to cook them that evening. He knew a good sauce for mackerel, he said. I found him later in the galley with steam around his head and butter spitting at him, every pan in use and a couple of empty tins as well. Alice darkened the companionway for a moment, saying 'I thought *maquereau a la facon de Quimper* was a simple dish.' At this point he opened a box of matches upside down. His face was red from the heat of the galley. I picked up the matches and promised to help wash the pots.

He brought the food to the table saying it was a disaster with no fresh herbs, though we truly enjoyed it. He was very quiet when we washed up and there was no literary discussion. I felt able to look at him at close quarters – without fearing either his beauty or his academic energy. I felt protective and said,

'Do you have any of your poems with you? I'd like to see them.'

He paused. It was as if he was trying to decide if I would take one of his poems and break its neck.

'They're very slight, but yes, come to my quarters.' Laughing at this exaggerated air of conspiracy, he fetched a folder from his berth and we went on deck. The rain had held off but the clouds seemed very low and with no wind you could hear sounds far across the moorings. Outboard engines, a radio signature tune, the splash of a bucket plunged overboard. The wash from a passing boat made the dinghy bump against the side of 'Grey Goose' and the rigging slapped against the mast over our heads. Alice and Alastair were talking quietly in the cabin. Martin sat on the forehatch and began; I sat sideways to him looking down at the grain of the deck. I was prepared to be polite. I felt I had been grudging in our academic conversations. Now I would temper critical remarks with praise for which I was determined to find cause.

He pretended to look self-important. 'Shall I wait for silence?' as a gull screeched above us.

What had I expected? Something abstruse and cerebral and full of literary allusions I suppose. The poems were delicate. I'd say 'finely carved' but the impression was more of movement, a constant shimmer. There were hard clear images but the feelings attached to them came from beyond normal consciousness. It was both strange and peculiar. A razor shell in the mud at low tide turns out to be an ivory fan. Natural objects and human artefacts were subtly linked. A shell seemed sculpted, a cup might have been turned by the wind, a jug took its lustre from the rain.

They were such a gift that I didn't allow my guilt to stay around too long. I tried to forget I had been so patronizing. It was a joy to listen and then afterwards to talk about them, although now he was the reluctant one. 'I should have known from the way you reacted to our bluebells,' I said.

'Why?'

'The metamorphosis. The way they became something else.'

'I think what appealed to me was you and Alice, the idea of you together all those years ago.'

That night I asked Alice why she hadn't told me about Martin's poetry.

'I was afraid it might put you off.' I had underestimated her too.

*   *   *

I was nearly asleep when the idea came. There had been the scent of recognition for me in one of his poems, a bare foot on a sand dune at dawn feeling the sand cold and treading on spiky grass. Somehow it linked with a memory of mine and this became an incident in the life of a person who was not me. The dunes were outside a town where the street lights burned on as dawn came and seagulls flew very low or strutted down the middle of empty streets.

It went on and I was thinking I would write it down but I fell asleep.

The next morning it was still there and growing. I felt very awake with sharpened senses. From the next cabin I could smell the gas and hear the kettle beginning its slow ticking and rasping towards a boil. I had no paper. I had to shape it all in my head. I believed in it, it had life.

I wanted to drink my tea alone so I could think over the story, even rejoice in its existence. But there was no sneaking away. In the main cabin, Alastair said, 'You're looking well, Sal. What do you think, Alice, is it love?'

'Alastair!'

'Sorry, sorry. The forecast says light to moderate SW breezes today. Will we make Falmouth?'

My ideal would have been for everyone to go ashore while I stayed on board and got writing.

'Anyone got any paper?' I asked as casually as possible.

'What for?' said Alice sharply.

'Oh nothing much.'

'Martin's sure to have some. Is it for a letter?'

'Sort of.'

I couldn't tell her, not at that stage. Later on it seemed my wish would be answered. There was to be a shore party, I said I'd stay behind. Martin had given me some paper and promised to buy some in town. He treated the desire for paper as too normal for comment. He also treated me as an equal, a friend, neither an object of deference nor a mangler of mackerel.

At the last minute, Alice decided to stay with me for

company. We spent our time sweeping the cabin floor, airing sleeping bags and cleaning the cooker. I didn't tell her about the story.

Martin brought the paper. We set off for Falmouth. Light to moderate breezes became moderate to fresh. Now I had a story in my head, plenty of paper and nowhere to write. The deck was sloping, the chart table was sloping and the cockpit was full of our bodies. Objects in the galley slid and crashed. I told the story to stay where it was and sat in the cockpit feeling the sun and looking at the dark blue sea. Alastair decided it was a day for sea shanties. He would take the verse, we sang the refrain. And so across St Austell Bay I uttered such words as 'Away, haul away' without disturbing the shape or details of what was suspended within me.

Once we arrived in Falmouth it was harder. Too much was going on. I became irritable. A plan started to form as undeniable as the story. I would have to return home. It occurred to me to go ashore, ring a neighbour and discover that my flat had been burgled, but it felt bad enough leaving them without lying too.

I was going to tell Martin but then imagination got to work and I fancied him saying 'But that's wonderful! Let me help. I'll take the others off somewhere.' And then he'd want to see it. Would the story warrant all that fuss and secrecy? It was always the same. I had something growing in my mind which had its own independent shape. I took pleasure in its energy. There were no doubts. But then came the practicalities: paper, space, now a train timetable and because I felt like a child in these matters I was unable to service my own inspiration. Perhaps Shakespeare and Wordsworth and Emily Dickinson were not strangely inspired, perhaps they were simply very competent.

I didn't tell Martin about the story but I did confide first in him saying I had to go home and would explain later. He was very cast down. 'Is it to do with the university? Some family thing?'

'I'll explain. Really. I'll write to you.'

It was hardest telling Alice.

'But what is it? Why can't you explain?' I felt terrible. The less she understood the harder it would be to explain the truth. Even till the end I thought I might. But she didn't see writing as something that got in the way of arrangements.

'I have enjoyed it. I've loved being with you all. It's just that I have to go now.'

Alice came to me when I was in my bunk. 'Sal, is it anything to do with Martin?'

'No, well maybe indirectly. I'll write and explain, really. Thanks for everything. Thanks for having me. It's done me a lot of good.'

I was sleeping in the forward cabin with the sails and the anchor chain. Later, after dark, I pushed up the hatch and looked out at the harbour. Lights shone on the water from other boats and from the streets. Falmouth always seemed to smell of rotting onions along with fuel oil and seaweed, and yet I loved it. I breathed deeply and indulged the sense of how I would have liked to stay as I listened to voices and music on the water. Martin was still reading under his canvas awning. Perhaps he was writing a poem. I thought of James Joyce writing *Ulysses* on the top of a suitcase in a Paris hotel.

Alastair rowed me ashore the next day and I repeated my thanks. I don't believe he minded. Just as we were pushing away from 'Grey Goose' Alice came to the side and called, 'Oh Sally, I haven't had a chance to say goodbye.'

These words came back to me on the train. They seemed especially weighted. I started a fearful fantasy that she was dying and had never told me and now never would. There was rain on the train windows. *Desolation Island* lay unopened on my knee. I thought about Martin and imagined inviting him to read at the university Poetry Society. I could handle admiring his poetry more easily than being disconcerted by his good looks. All the same I had used him or used an image from his poem and then moved on.

When I got home the flat was very calm and empty. I had stopped at the corner shop and now, because they didn't sell tinned macaroni cheese, I cooked pasta and didn't let it froth over. At the same time I carefully made a white sauce and added grated cheese. Tomorrow I would buy a wooden spoon.

After eating I cleared the table and wiped away all crumbs, then set out pen and paper. But before sitting down I washed the dishes and both saucepans. The crockery squeaked. I used what I had, fingers and thumbs.

THE PINK PEIGNOIR

There she was walking ahead of him on the road. All day he had been getting lifts with farmers, people whose clothes were chosen not to stand out. She was wearing an out-dated Indian skirt and walking in that erect, gracious way of hers as though she was someone special. He stayed behind her till she turned in at the gate. When she saw him she looked pleased but not in the least surprised. And yet it was five years now since he was last there. He saw that her hair was grey where she had pulled it back. Her two small children were brown but her pallor was as striking as ever.

'I see you've turf in your fingernails,' he said as she handed him tea.

'Black olives. From making the children's pizza.'

They were always restful in each other's company. She saw him gazing out through the kitchen window. There was a barn with rough stone walls and a corrugated iron roof still showing traces of faded red paint. A pile of rose-rust ashes, dust from many turf fires, had been spilled over a clump of nettles. You could see the mountains in the distance and in the foreground a hawthorn hedge. One bush was white with blossom, the rest were draped with clothes and sheets.

'The washing line broke,' she laughed, 'We're like the tinkers.'

'You wouldn't last twenty-four hours with them.' He'd said it years before when he'd suspected her of playing the Lady to his raggle-taggle gipsy.

Suddenly she left the room, saying, 'I was tidying up' and came back with what looked like a bundle of pink rags.

'Do you remember it?'

He did. She shook it out, a light gown, peachy-pink made of flimsy thin cotton. He remembered a cottage they once stayed in with cobwebs in the windows but no curtains. At once he was back with cracked lino under bare feet, gulping cold spring water and the smell of her skin.

'It was the shortest night of the year, remember?'

'What did you call that thing again?'

'It's a peignoir. Pain wire.'

He smiled but would not say it. They had pinned it up against the long hours of light. It was dim and sensuous and they made love in its glow. Afterwards she spoke about the way the light brought out the white flowers embroidered on it, 'like a stained glass window.' But already his mind had been on his journey. She was only out of hospital for the weekend; he had taken her from Occupational Therapy where she was weaving the bright plastic seat of a stool. Taking her back, he had worried against his will that this had been bad for her.

'No! It's been lovely. The best thing. You took away the pain wire from around my brain.'

Now he began to have doubts again about her mental state as she handed the garment to him saying, 'Take it. It's torn beyond repair, I can't wear it. I want you to have it.'

He stuffed it in his back-pack. 'Are you well these days?'

'Fine. I wonder would you help me fix the clothes-line?'

He left in the evening still some hours before dark.

'Stay longer next time.'

'Just don't ask me to paint the roof of the barn.'

It was still light when he reached the end of the peninsula. He had felt uneasy hitching lifts, thinking of the tattered pink garment in his pack. Now he walked an empty road between stretches of turf on one side and the sea on the other, the dark side darkening and the light seeming to get lighter. He came to many crossroads but no signposts. As dusk came the whin bushes pulsed gold, aggressive, beautiful. At one of the crossroads he swung down his back-pack and took out the peignoir. Tenderly he spread it over a thorn bush. If he returned that way it might still be there; it would help mark the journey.

Looking back from higher ground he saw how it glimmered. It was almost the colour of the pink may blossom. Maybe a breeze would lift it and take it away.

INSIDE

I am a hostage. I'm scared. I don't know how I got here but there was violence. I remember a lot of fighting. I'm very scared. But I must not panic. I must keep my head. I need to work things out.

This room is dark. I've tried the door and of course it's locked. There's a bed in here that's all. There's also a window but it has a sort of shutter on the inside, a solid board. This is also locked. I reached up and there was a keyhole.

It's very hot. They've taken my clothes and I'm wearing some kind of tunic. I can't see it but I can feel it coarse against my skin. It smells bad, sweet and sickly.

I sit on the bed. There's just one cover. I'm on the edge of the bed keeping my feet on the floor. My feet are bare. I keep them on the ground because it feels safer.

I'm trying to think. Where was I seized? Jack and I

were at the airport. We were going to Morocco for a late summer holiday. There was some kind of a row at the airport. My head aches trying to think about it.

Jack must be here too. They wouldn't have taken me without him. Someone will negotiate for him. But what about me? Who do I have value for? I don't have any. I have no role, no profession. And of course no children.

I listen. At least my heart has stopped thumping now. There's no sound at all from outside. No voices, no footsteps.

Who will they negotiate with? The government will surely try to get Jack freed. Perhaps as his wife I can be part of the deal. I would never have wanted that before. I'm an independent woman. But I'm scared now. For being of no value they might kill me.

I lay back on the bed and I must have fallen asleep. I wake up terrified but force myself to be calm. Things look a bit different now. A tiny sliver of grey light has appeared round the edges of the window board. The keyhole shows very clearly. It's too high for me to look through so I move the bed to the window and by kneeling on it I can squint through to the outside. I'm excited, but all I can see is part of a white wall opposite and a door. A large black bird flies past. It looks like a crow. I don't learn anything. The wall and the door, which is a faded red, and the crow could be anywhere.

But while I've my eye screwed up to peer out, fresh air comes to my nostrils. It smells wonderful. Just ordinary, but of the outside and of the very early morning. I put my nose to the keyhole and breathe in as if I can draw life from it.

I can hear noises in the distance. Voices. They don't seem to be speaking low or secretively. What is this place? I hope someone will come to speak to me but at the same time I dread it.

I make sure I have my feet on the ground. I pace about, my stomach sinking as sounds come nearer. Then the door is unlocked and bursts open and a boy comes in, puts something on the ground and unlocks the window board. Light crashes round the walls. He goes quickly to the door again. He makes sure not to come near me. It's as though he's frightened of me. He must be about twelve, black-haired, dark-featured. He locks the door after him.

The bowl of food he's left on the floor could be anything – rice, wheat, couscous. I look closely and it smells like porridge. Anyway I won't be eating it. They tried to poison me last night.

Now I can see out of the window. It's barred. What is this place? The bars look as if they've always been there. It's no makeshift arrangement but some kind of regular holding centre.

I see now the thing I'm wearing is a dull green, some kind of regulation garment like a uniform. The bed cover is the same kind of green. The walls are cream, plain and undecorated and the floor seems to be lino made to look like wood.

There's not much to see through the window, just a wider view of the wall and the door. But now I see it's a mural, a lighthouse and headland has been painted in white on a reddish brick background. It reminds me of somewhere. The door looks as if it's never open. A few long grasses grow at the base of the wall and there's a small patch of green which could be the corner of a lawn. I'm having to stretch up to see all this so I move the bed again and kneel on it, staring out. Nothing moves, but I don't give up. Something has raised my hopes. It may be the daylight or the ordinariness of the wall and the door and the grasses at the foot of the wall. Even the painted lighthouse suggests human activity.

I won't go so far as to say there's a hint of normality; I'm in a locked room looking out through bars.

Nobody comes. The food is cold now and I'm hungry but I won't touch it. Last night they tried to make me drink a sweet-smelling red potion. I tossed it away. I think that's what's spilt on my garment. Now it's sticky and vile-smelling.

Jack comes into my mind and he seems far away already. He's in another life. But surely he is here too and he must be worried about me. I must try to make contact. I can't risk calling his name but I decide to sing to him. Something he'll know is me, that will lift his spirits, nothing wistful. I'm scared but I open my mouth and I sing Blanche's song when she's singing in the bath.

> *It's a Barnum and Bailey world*
> *Just as something as it can be.*
> *But it wouldn't be make-believe*
> *If you believed in me.*

After the first line I was confident. There's just my voice, strong and loud. No one comes to stop me. I carry on louder with the bits I remember,

> *Without your love*
> *It's a honkey tonk parade*
> *Without your love...*

Now I hear knocking and banging in the distance and yelling but I don't hear Jack. *Without your love...* Someone crashes against my door and tries to open it – *Without your love it's a honkey tonk parade* – then unlocks the door and in comes the young boy. But now it seems he's not a boy at all but a girl wearing a blue dress with a belt. She's looking very flustered. With her is a large-boned fair woman in the same kind of dress but a darker blue. She starts to yell at me in a loud Australian accent,

'Be quiet! You can't make that noise! You're

disturbing other people.' She comes right into my cell and pushes the bed back into place. 'You must calm down now, Jeannie.'

So she knows my name?

She and the young dark one have a whispering session, something about 'seeing Ahmed'. As they leave, the dark one turns nervously to me and puts a finger to her lips as if to say 'hush' to a child.

Well I know how to get their attention now, but do I want it? And who are the 'other people' who must not be disturbed? One thing, they don't seem to be planning to kill me. Not yet, anyway.

*   *   *

I've discovered something absolutely amazing. They've got that stolen picture here! The one by Munch, 'The Scream' I think it's called, with the woman on the bridge screaming in anguish. I found it when I was moving the bed out again. It was hidden in the corner wrapped in a tunic like mine only torn and dusty. It has been put in a different frame. This is a cheap, would-be gilt – totally unsuitable. I feel very shaky. It's amazing to have discovered it but what should I do? Who knows it's in this room? I want to tell the whole world but of course I'm silenced. I wrap it up again and hide it under the bed.

42

Now there's a problem. If I want to look out of the window I need to move the bed but then I risk exposing the picture's hiding place. It seems to be the picture or the outside world. I will have to move the bed and the picture along with it. Ha! For an hour or so I had been beginning to think there was a horrible simplicity to the life of a hostage. Now it's getting as complicated as the outside world.

Then I have a great idea. I hide the picture under the mattress. But first I take a good look at it, keeping it hidden from the door. Oh I know how it feels, that scream. It's the whole person and the sky like blood and the bridge. The whole world is in desperation. I've known that scream all right. Now, though, it calms me. The whole business steadies me, finding it, recognising it, working out how to hide it. The only thing that feels wrong is looking at it alone. Is that to be its fate, to be looked at in secrecy by some rich collector?

All this has stopped me feeling so scared. But now there are voices outside the door and somebody knocks. I don't answer. It's sheer mockery to imprison me and then knock on my door.

It opens and in comes Big Australian Bully with a tall dark man – Middle Eastern I think – and the little dark Nice Girl. Something in the body language of the three of them tells me he is important. One of their leading figures, I assume. He looks serious. His fanaticism is well under control. His question is like the knock on the door.

'How are you feeling today?'

'How do you think? Confined, imprisoned. I don't want to be here. I am of no value to you. I want to be let go.'

'On the contrary, you are of value. All here are of value.'

He starts muttering to Big Australian.

I speak again. 'Where is my husband? I want to see my husband.'

They mutter again and he states, 'You will see your husband.'

They turn to go and with the same serious expression he says, 'I hear you like to sing. You may sing but quietly, you understand?' His two companions smile but not at me.

After they've gone I lie on the bed with clenched fists pounding the mattress. I am furious at my own docility. I have allowed his presence to overpower me. I should have argued, persuaded, even pleaded. But I allowed myself to be drawn into the spell of his authority.

I take out the picture and let it do the screaming for me. The frame bothers me. And the painting itself seems oddly smooth in texture, almost like a reproduction. I'm puzzling over this when Nice Girl comes in without knocking. Seeing the picture she gasps.

'Where did you get that?'

I tell her. She holds out her hand gently and I give it to her.

'You must not have,' she says, so I snatch it back. Out she goes, returning almost at once with Big Australian who must have been told to be nice to me because she's very sweet and reasonable.

'This is not supposed to be here. It has been decided it isn't suitable in a place like this. I'll find you a better one.'

She takes 'The Scream' from me and they both leave, saying 'Lunchtime soon'.

How odd, I'm thinking. 'Lunchtime'?

Nice Girl comes in a little later with a small glass of the red poison and some water.

'No thanks,' I say firmly.

'Then you will not be allowed lunch,' she says trying to look fierce.

'I don't give a damn,' I say, 'I'm not drinking that.'

After she's gone I sniff the red stuff. It's the same as was spilled on my tunic all right. No thanks.

I look forlornly out at the white wall and the once-red door and the grasses. I need to go to the bathroom. I'm quite uncomfortable by the time Big Australian comes bursting in.

'Dr Ahmed says you have to take your medication.'

'I need the toilet.'

She has brought another glass of water and a large white tablet. I make a show of swallowing this, tossing back my head but depositing it in my cheek.

'Good girl. That wasn't so bad was it?'

I've heard that before.

She takes me across the corridor to the toilet. I flush away the tablet. It is when I am returning to the room, mid-way in the corridor that a smell hits me. Something I've known before. Reminding me of another place and a distant feeling.

I lie on my bed and think about the 'medication'. I'm imagining some strange, dark chemical process whereby Ahmed re-arranges and sedates our minds. But it's all very unconvincing and science fiction-y because at the same time my thoughts are whirling in a panic at another possibility and one that is far more likely.

What kind of a place is this?

There's a squeak of wheels outside the room, a loud knock and a cry of 'tea!' The door opens and I see the lady with the tea-trolley. There is the large shiny teapot, the jug of milk, the cups and saucers and the tin of biscuits.

'Yes please,' I say and gaze at this familiar sight.

'Sugar, darlin'?' she asks, and now I know where I am.

She hands me a cup of tea and there are two bourbon biscuits on the saucer.

I don't want her to go. I need to know exactly which place this is. But I would feel a fool showing that I don't know. So I can only say 'thanks' and she goes, taking certainty and knowledge with her.

If I am where I think I am it's even more urgent that I get out. Sheer panic assaults me when I realise the truth. All the rest of my thinking was fantasy – or was it? Now my mind starts to play back along with the fantasies. The smell in the corridor is a hospital smell. The tea-lady is the hospital tea-lady. But They could have arranged all this to deceive me.

When Nice Girl comes in again I ask her directly, 'Are you a nurse?'

'No not exactly. I am in training.'

Training, training. As what?

'Do you expect to become a nurse?'

'Oh yes. And you must help me.'

'How can I help you?'

'By being a good patient and taking your medication and being calm and good.'

I don't want to spoil her prospects but when Big Aussie comes in with the replacement picture I behave like a proper mental hospital patient.

'This is much nicer,' she says, showing me something mostly brown with a flat pond and ducks and reeds.

'Take the disgusting thing away!'

I scream and throw it across the room.

I've surprised her, I think, because all she can say is 'Well!' and she leaves the room locking the door noisily behind her.

For a moment I remember the exhilaration of madness, the power it can give you. But I'm not mad. Not this time.

Now I'm even more anxious to know how I got here. And my mind has accepted where I am, linking together 'Dr' Ahmed, the smell, 'lunch-time', the tea-trolley. But it won't quite abandon the idea that I'm a hostage and these people are my captors.

Lunch comes. It's brought by the tea-lady. 'Do you not have a locker?' she asks, standing there with a plate of stew in her hands.

Then she puts it on the bed and leaves, saying I need a locker. It's a comforting thought. I'll be given a locker and there will be a jug of water and a glass on top and some pieces of fruit and then inside a few personal items, underwear and a towel and a notebook.

The stew is unmistakeably Irish. Plenty of potatoes and a few bits of unknown meat. I'm hungry and eat it all.

There's a gentle knock on the door. Nice Girl comes in. She's Nice Nurse now. She approaches tentatively. I see her looking at the rejected picture on the floor. Its frame has survived the fall. It's the same kind of ersatz gilt as they'd put on the Munch.

'I need a locker,' I say.

'I will tell. Of course you must have.'

She seems reassured by my demand. 'But now. Your fingernails.'

'What?' I look at my nails for the first time in what seems like ages. 'They're not very long.'

'No, but too sharp. It will be nice. You see.'

She sits on the bed. 'Come.' She has a pair of nail scissors.

'Why do I have to have my nails cut?'

'See!' She shows me the back of her hand and the arm above the wrist. 'You did.'

There are red scratch marks, some quite deep.

'I did that?'

She nods.

'Oh I'm sorry. I didn't know. I thought you were bad people trying to imprison me.' Of course I'm sorry but I have no recollection of this and it's as though I'm being blamed for what I've done in someone else's dream.

'No we are good people. This is a good place. Now.'

While shame and forgetfulness have brought down my defences she takes me by the hand and sits me on the bed beside her. Very carefully and gently she takes my fingers and clips each nail, talking soothingly as to a child. 'There this is a pretty one, this is a little tough, I think,' and so on. At first I am stiff and flinch but then begin to relax. I look sideways at the dark eyelashes against dark skin and the brow puckered in concentration. I am almost sorry when the job is done.

'There Jeannie. Not wild cat any more.'

'Thank you. Tell me, what is your name?'

What she says sounds like Chimaera.

'Ah that's a pretty name. Don't go I want to ask you something.'

'OK'

'Why am I here? Do you know?'

'Because you are sick. You need to rest.'

'I can't remember coming in. What do you know about it?'

'Your husband. He was worried.'

'But why?'

She's looking awkward now.

'Chimaera. Don't you think I have the right to know?'

'You tried to run away. At the airport.'

'Really? I tried to run away?'

'Yes, I believe you tried to get on a different plane. Then you got angry when they wouldn't let you and you had a bad fight with the people at the airport.'

'OK don't tell me any more.'

'You wanted to go to America.'

I remember nothing of this. She could have been making it up. But in some distant part of my mind it does remind me of something.

How tiring this is! As she leaves she says, 'You are nice to let me do your nails. Later I help you have a bath and I will see you get a locker.'

And a chair, an armchair in the corner, I think, with sinking heart.

I try to process Chimaera's information but it hardly seems connected with me. I lie on the bed and look at the sky which is absolutely pale like an empty page. I take another look out at the wall opposite, the door and the patch of grass. I wonder what's round the corner. It would be good to see trees and water. I feel the world has been taken away from me even though really it's me that's been taken away from it.

Later Chimaera takes me to bathe in a room with shiny yellow walls and a high window. She becomes quite playful, pretending not to hear my commands about the hot and cold taps.

Her hair is getting in her face and eyes, she's indiscriminately splashing and laughing. For the first time in weeks, I notice another person's mood.

'You seem happy,' I say and she tells me she is going off duty for ten days. 'You won't be here when I come back,' she says and it's a little while before I realise what she means, that I am part of a timetable in the real world.

I am given a clean nightdress. It's a washed-out pale blue and softer than the one I've been wearing. It's quite easy for Chimaera to give me my tablet now. There are sheets on the bed. I try not to think about Jack because I know I have embarrassed and hurt him. I fall asleep easily.

*   *   *

I wake and remember where I am and that Jack is not here. They don't board up my window now. The morning sun shines on the wall opposite and I see that the lighthouse is not painted on at all. It's just that white paint has flaked off and left behind a shape that looks like a lighthouse. I feel worse now. This is not the scary adventure I thought it was but it's still frightening in its own way. Also when the door knocks and someone comes in, of course it's not Chimaera. This one has mousy hair and a plain face. She seems very off-hand, her English perfect when she asks if I want toast this morning. I say

'Sure', but that what I really want is paper to write a letter. Toast comes but no paper. I take my tablet. I remember what it's like in a place like this: they will bring you porridge, tea and tablets but you may wait forever for a piece of paper.

I look out and the sun is very bright now. It dazzles on the white part of the wall opposite. I see the red bricks clearly, they have weeds and moss growing between them. Some familiar-looking birds are pecking about on the patch of grass. I feel stupid when I remember what I thought this place was. And yet there still comes into my mind the idea of something sinister. It's true that I've realised about the white paint and that no one has actually painted a lighthouse. But the red door is still strange. It's always closed. What is it hiding?

Maybe she's not so bad, the English one. She brings paper and when I start to ask 'Pen?' sarcastically, she says 'Oh sorry,' and lends me her own.

I try to write to Jack. My writing is very shaky and I find it extremely difficult to form sentences. It's as if my mind is racing too much and at the same time is far too slow to catch up with itself. It's like two totally un-matched ponies trying to pull a cart.

The letter is quite short. I fold it up and put it under my pillow. Now the day lies ahead of me with the huge task of requesting and eventually, I hope, obtaining an envelope and then finding some way to post it. The odd thing is that as soon as I've hidden away the letter I completely forget what I've said in it. I don't bother to look. I just know I've begged him to get me out of here.

Then Big Australian comes in. Breezes in, I should say, with to me meaningless enquiries after my health. Why is she still here if Chimaera's gone, I wonder. She's pleased with herself. 'Look what came for you!' and hands me a package. She fusses with my bed and finds the letter.

'I need an envelope.' I say, turning the package over in my hands.

'Please,' she can't stop herself saying as she leaves, 'Please may I have an envelope.'

I recognise Jack's writing of course, and his style of neatly re-using old envelopes and the address label on the back.

He's sent me a new night-dress, a bought one. It's pretty in a summery, flowery way. I unfold it and see that it has short sleeves and a high neck. It smells of fresh cotton. I suppose he couldn't send my favourite, an old jellaba torn under one arm, or his favourite, the skimpy black. There's a letter, a note rather. It's pretty skimpy itself with only two real sentences, 'I hope you are feeling better' and 'I'll come and visit you soon.'

Australia comes back quickly with an envelope. 'Nice surprise?' she asks, indicating the package.

54

I'm trying not to cry because he hasn't said he misses me and there's nothing about rescuing me. So I don't speak and so she goes out again, saying, 'You know your door's not locked now so you can go to the bathroom. But don't go wandering off because we can see you from the nurses' station.'

I feel like a child. The grown-ups have left me in the care of strangers.

A few minutes ago I was trying not to cry and now I can't. I lie on the bed. It's morning but I'm exhausted already. I fall asleep, reminding myself that Jack has always been 'a man of few words.' And so very, very normal.

The tea-trolley wakes me. After it's gone I leave my door open and listen to it trundling and squeaking away and then to the other noises of the ward. There seems to be a communal area beyond the nurses' station because every so often screams of laughter come from that direction. It's high-pitched and sometimes desperate but I envy the laughers without wanting to join them. I'm sitting on the bed with the door open when a very tall, fair-haired woman about my age appears outside. She wears a vivid pink night-gown and is sliding along the wall opposite, pressed against the wall and shrinking as if from blows or threats of blows. Her whole body signals distress. She's acting out the despair I sometimes feel the way Munch's picture did. I'm paralysed but I feel I should help her. By the time I get to my feet and look out she's gone.

I drink my tea and put the letter in the envelope and address it. Of course I have no money for a stamp and it bothers me that I'll have to ask someone to post it.

The tablets must be making me drowsy. I sleep again and dream that I am strong and wearing my clothes and I'm conducting an orchestra. I'm in control but all the time I have to listen hard to know what they're playing. I wake to the sound of Ravel's 'Bolero' quite near. Then there's someone shouting and the music is the bit where it's so unmistakeably yearning. Abruptly the sound is gone and a wail of anger is followed by Australian nurse's voice saying, 'I told you, Jennifer.' I look out and see a young girl being shepherded along the corridor towards the communal noise. I look both ways, hoping to see the one in the pink nightie but there is no sign of her. I'm feeling very shaky and upset now and when I wonder how soon before I will get out, I feel completely helpless.

There are noises outside my window. There's a loud clattering, a sound of wood hitting wood and men's voices. The door in the wall opposite is open! They are hauling deckchairs, lots of them, out of the darkness and leaning them against the wall. The canvas is bright and colourful against the faded paint. Then they are carried out of my sight. The door is left casually open.

There's a lot going on today. Visitors come. I hear voices in the corridor and groups of people pass, talking in even, normal tones or in tones slightly buffed up into cheerfulness.

I wait in the room for Jack. I have tidied the bed. My newly cut nails still have an edge to them as they press into my palms. Perhaps if I go for a walk I will meet him. I hope there won't be anyone else with him.

I wander down the corridor past the nurses' station. There is no-one there. Sunlight is coming into the building. Long windows have been opened and outside them on the edge of the garden are the deck-chairs and women sitting in them. Some wear dressing-gowns in different bright colours. Others wear their clothes. They all have sun-hats on. They call to each other and laugh. They know each other's names.

The sun is very bright out there. I see that the garden has a large lawn and flower-beds.

I don't want to be seen. I don't know anyone. I go back to my room. It seems almost dark here now. The sun has left the wall opposite.

*   *   *

Jack doesn't come. I hear other people's visitors leaving. Outside my window the red door is still open showing a dark emptiness.

When my door opens it's two nurses, laughing and wheeling in a bed-side locker. One is the English nurse from this morning. There are red streaks in her hair now.

'Thanks,' I say. 'I need a stamp for my letter. Please.'

'If you want to give me the letter, I'll post it for you.'

'Do you recognise her?' asks the other, giggling.

'Sure, why wouldn't I?' I take the letter from under my pillow and hand it to her. 'Thanks.'

'Do you like her hair?'

'It's OK'

'Ahmed won't approve,' and they leave, still laughing.

I have a locker now but nothing to put in it. Then I remember the pen under my pillow and open the drawer of the locker and put it in.

A little later, on top of the locker there is a plate of ham salad which I have not touched. I'm very restless. I wish Chimaera were here.

I wander into the corridor. Once again the nurses' station is empty. I hear Red Streaks and the other laughing in someone's room. This time they're getting a response. I come to the French windows. The deck-chairs are all empty now. A fallen leaf is lying on one. There are cigarette ends on the ground between them. I walk out past them to the lawn. It's sunny still but now the trees make long shadows. The grass feels lovely under my bare feet. I walk to the trees and shiver because it's nearly Autumn and my arms are bare. I look back at the deck-chairs. Their colours are blurry and jumbled together like in some warm Impressionist painting. And the flower beds glow, all yellows and deep reds. I go to look closely at the flowers and smell them and I hear bees making that rich, comfortable sound. There comes a moment of sudden joy and my eyes fill with tears. But then I sneeze and a nurse passing the windows sees me. She comes out looking cross until she notices my tears and puts an arm round me.

'You're cold. You'll catch your death. You can't come out here without your clothes.'

'I haven't got my clothes,' and I encourage my tears a little.

'Oh, we'll see about that. You must stay inside now.'

When I get back to my room, the patient in the pink nightie is there leaning on the wall near my door. She shrinks as I approach.

'It's all right, I won't hurt you,' I say.

'I know.' Then she comes close and whispers, 'Do you want to come swimming?'

'Swimming? Where?'

'Here. Look.'

She starts to slide along the wall, moving her arms and

legs together as if in side-stroke. 'Come on, it's lovely!'

I lean against the wall beside her and stretch my arms along it.

'That's right, you've got it!'

The floor is shiny too.

She no longer looks wounded but is beginning to laugh. 'Come on! Keep up!'

Now I'm laughing too. It's a conspiracy of the mad. We are both gasping with laughter and breathless as we move along the wall.

At the end of the corridor we come to a closed door. 'That's where they put the men,' she whispers, 'I'm glad they're locked away.'

'Well I enjoyed that,' she says, quite formally as if we'd just taken a turn round the grounds together. She puts out her hand as if to shake mine, then changes her mind. 'I must go back to the sitting-room now. I have some knitting to attend to.' I want her to speak to me. She has ended our encounter too quickly.

But back in my room I lie on my bed and smile at the thought of our crazy swim. Outside there's a clatter and bang as the deck-chairs are put away and the door closed on them.

I look back over the day. It's true that Jack did not come. But I have obtained a sheet of paper and written a letter, and I have requested and received an envelope and arranged for the letter to be posted.   I have walked in the garden and swum in the corridor.   I will soon be getting my clothes back.

Tomorrow I will negotiate my release.

ALLIANCES

'Why does it feel like Christmas?' My brother asked.

It was a bright October day. We were in Cornwall, in the house we had grown up from. Our father was in hospital; our mother sat with him. He was dying. James and I had seen him very early that morning. His eyes had been closed and he breathed like a sail flapping in the wind.

I thought about what James had said.

'Yes, I suppose it does. Why, though?'

'I'm not sure. There's plenty of drink in the house. A fire… And we're waiting.'

'That's it. And the weather.'

We had a good fire going. Coal, and some wood from a dead apple tree. I watched the flames shrivel grey lichen. James took out his Old Holborn tin.

'Still smoking?' I said for form's sake, sisterly.

'Filthy Disgusting Habit,' his reply was equally automatic.

He went to the sideboard.

'Only with a drink these days, actually, what do you want?'

'I don't know. Drinking in the mornings always makes me... OK I'll have some brandy.'

'There's no sloe gin of course.'

'That's right, no sloe gin.'

'No Cidrax for us kids.'

'No nuts, no tangerines.'

'No long oval flat packs of dates with sticky palm trees on the top.'

'No Brussels sprouts.'

'No Crown Derby to break the gravy dish of.'

'You did that!'

'Yes, but I mended it with Araldite.'

The sun shone on the fire, quenching it as we stared.

'It is also the weather,' I said again, looking at the brandy in its dusty glass, 'remember how it would be wind and rain up till Christmas and then the wind dropped and Christmas Day was always clear and sunny?'

'And we had to go for a walk on the beach before dinner.'

'Lucky you. I had to sit in the kitchen and do the

sprouts. And carrots. And rub stale bread together to make crumbs.'

There was a pause. James was shredding a very small amount of tobacco between his fingers.

'What was that for?'

'Bread sauce.'

'Ah. Then we came back and it was never ready so we kind of stood and sat around cracking nuts.'

'Dad would come into the kitchen and offer to help, but it was the range. When the wind dropped it got slow and sulked and he could never revive it.'

James groaned and the groan changed to a sigh of pity.

'I was remembering how he could skim stones. Ten, twelve leaps to my two or three. I practised all summer but on Christmas Day – plop! One plop and down. His used to leap along the water for him.'

'He must have practised.'

'Yeah he believed in that.'

'Still does I suppose.'

We both looked at the clock, a round-shouldered clunky thing from the thirties. For nearly all our childhood it had been stuck at twenty past twelve. Then our sister, Penny, on a visit back from the Home Counties had taken it to a watch-maker and had it fixed. Our mother viewed this as a miracle.

'It's what people do,' said Penny.

James pinched the tobacco from each end of his thin cigarette. When he struck the match I closed my eyes and breathed in gently. This is what home meant now, his smoke and the ever-renewing patterns of our minds, nibbling at memories, eroding and rebuilding allegiances, being honest about all kinds of things we'd hidden out of kindness or shame. Sometimes I'd seen him give a quick glance at our two nieces, offspring of Penny and 'that pillock Randallson' but I wasn't sure what he was thinking. So far we hadn't talked about that, about neither of us having children. His girlfriend was still young. We both enjoyed local gossip, unlike our parents who had come from other places.

Now he said, 'You know who's in the same ward as him?'

'No. Excite me.' For that moment I strayed from honesty, the hard-bitten manner disguising the panic that gripped me when he mentioned the ward.

'Old Harry Morgan,' and then at my blank look, 'You know. Mr Morgan. The farmer.'

'Oh Christ! Meany Morgan.'

'Was he that bad?'

'I'd no idea he was still alive.'

'He looked more alive than the rest of them, beady eyes

peeping out.'

'Oh I bet the nurses love him. Was there ever anyone so mean and grumpy and two-faced charming?'

'Why don't you like him?'

'Ask Penny, she'll tell you.'

'She won't remember him.'

'She will, she will. We both hated him.'

'What did he do? Grope you in the cowshed or something?'

'No. He set traps.'

'Traps! For you and Penny?'

'No, rabbit traps. You know.'

'Come on, no one used rabbit traps. Don't you remember myxomatosis?'

I tried not to remember a shaking creature, unable to move in a muddy lane and the bitter argument between me and Penny as to whether we should stone it to death to end its pain.

'No, it was before that.'

Then I told him about the small mounds of earth at the bottom of the sloping fields.

'They were like molehills only flatter. I can still see the pale clay, freshly tilled. Inside these heaps was a deadly spring trap. Tearful, indignant, Penny and I trudged from field to field and when we found a heap of earth would lightly press a foot on it till we heard and felt the sharp release of the spring. We were crammed with zeal, defenders of dumb creatures. The sensation beneath our feet became very satisfying. There's one! It's mine, it's my turn! Although we plodded to distant fields, it was Mr Morgan's land we covered most thoroughly.'

'Young fools! But you took a risk. I'd never have known it. Such a pair of goody-goodies. You could have lost a foot.'

'You only had to touch it lightly.' I flexed my ankle, remembering.

James laughed. 'Poor old Harry! He must have thought there were some damn clever rabbits about. Or did he catch you?'

'Well not... maybe. Dad found out. I told him actually. He was quoting that poem about the wretched blind pit ponies and the little hunted hares and saying we should respect animals and I volunteered how I was doing my bit – with Penny's help.'

James groaned. 'I bet he loved that. Local farmer, neighbour and all.'

'Yes, exactly. We were in deep disgrace. Interfering. Meddling in a Man's Livelihood and, and this I found hard to believe, putting ourselves in danger of losing a foot, being crippled for life.'

'Oh dear, oh dear. Little did I know. So it was weeding the garden or stay on the beach all day for you was it?'

'Just for a little while. I know we did collect a lot of shells.' On the table near the window the sun glinted on a bottle filled with whelks, cowries and razor shells.

'Then Penny got friendly with Cherry Ann Chenoweth so I was on my own.'

James peered through cigarette smoke into the distance. 'Cherry Ann Chenoweth. Blonde? Pony-tail?'

'Pony actually. That was the attraction.' I was reluctant to tell him the next bit. 'So I used to go down the Saddleback and find big enough stones and throw them at the traps.'

James was delighted as I thought he would be and that probably explains my reluctance. Those lonely days had held no pleasure for me. I was guilty and always nervous and I missed the thrilling vibration under my foot. Now, telling it, I thought of my father in the hospital, so much closer to Harry Morgan than us. I didn't want to be laughing at him. James had a different angle.

'Poor old Harry. He must have wondered what the hell was going on!' He stretched and got up and wandered to the sideboard and started fiddling with things. I wished he would sit down. I both wanted and didn't want to tell him the rest of the story.

'Do they use this soda siphon?' he asked and then, 'Good Lord there's actually some nuts here.'

'Let's see.   What kind?'

'They're sort of sheltering under a card of darning wool, and a Barclaycard and…'

'Show me.'

'They're those really hard ones no-one can ever crack.   I wonder what happened to the nutcrackers.'   He started opening drawers.   'Ah!'

'James!'   He was the irritating younger brother.

Taking his time, he came back to the fireside carrying a bowl and the whiskey bottle.   He put the bottle on the ground and the bowl, which now had the nutcrackers in it, on the chair.

'Back in a sec.'   He brought in more apple branches and a bottle of Gordon's about a third full.

'Why would this be in the laundry basket?'

'God knows.   What were you doing in the laundry basket?'

'Maybe that's where they keep the firewood, I thought. You'll have some gin?'

'Have you come across any tonic?'

'No, as far as I can see. No. Gin. Wasn't that what they called the traps?'

'Thanks but I won't. I used to hate the smell of it even. People drank it with orange. I can't think why.'

'But now?' He was prompting me in a slightly bored, distracted way, as though he'd heard it all before.

'Well now, of course, I like the tonic water to taste more and more of gin.'

'Ah, quite so.' He sat with the bowl on his lap and started to pick through it.

'Any treasures?' I asked. 'What's the red thing?'

It was a Father Christmas with icing on his feet. James put an almond between the jaws of the crackers and squeezed. Nothing happened.

'So. Did you manage to sabotage all the rabbit traps on the Rosinnis peninsula? With your stones which I trust you carried in a sling over your shoulder.'

He placed the bowl in the hearth and picked up the tobacco tin, opened it, took a sip of whiskey, a paper from the Rizla packet and settled himself for my story. I wanted to understate it and make it amusing. But there was too much fear and loneliness in it. It had been such a short incident; I was worried about being able to make it a good story.

I took a sip of brandy and said, 'Do you remember his tractor?' when James stopped with the cigarette uncompleted in his fingers, saying,

71

'I just remembered something! Did he come to our house for Christmas dinner one year? Yes! He sat in this chair.'

Of course I remembered. But to explain how I felt that day I'd have to go back to the time of the stones. James licked his paper. Or should I begin with the Christmas Day visit?

Then the phone rang. James immediately looked away and took on the day-dreaming gaze of one who hears the phone in a pub and knows the landlord will answer it.

We both expected it to be the hospital. I should answer it being the eldest. I stood up and knocked over the drink and was suddenly overwhelmed with tiredness. James looked at me then went to the phone. It was in the hall, just outside the door. My heart beat very fast. I looked round for something to mop up the brandy. I heard at once that it wasn't the hospital; he sounded familiar and a little guarded. Then he called, 'It's Penny,' and I made myself remember she was our ally. He was saying,

'No we were in the dining room... No, just talking... He's about the same, well, worse really. Whatever you want. Sure, stay with us – or here. Sal's found a bed here somewhere... Telling me stories about your heroic youth... No you may be right. But if not now, when is time? Want to speak to her? OK. Toodle-oo. See you.'

She didn't want to speak to me. When James observed that Randallson was probably in the background with a stop-watch and said she'd changed, somehow, Penny, I felt relieved. It was shameful to be pleased at our distance from Penny. We were incredulous at her values now. But I was also making up for the years when Penny had lived with a boozy outrageous friend of James and, until she had run for safety in the form of Thomas Randallson, I had felt excluded. I told myself I really would try to get through to her this time.

'When she's coming?'

'Oh whenever. Someone's got a swimming gala. Someone's got a music exam. Someone's playing in the Carnegie Hall. Sorry. Joking.' He filled our glasses and sat down.

'You were saying?'

'His tractor.'

'Right. No I can't say I remember it. Just a tractor like any other wasn't it?'

'You wouldn't think that if you'd been in my position. I used to see it parked in various fields and gateways. Penny and I used to think it looked a bit new-fangled because we knew his horses, Kerry and Sultan. Well, if I saw his tractor anywhere I'd keep clear. Lugging the stones was a bit of a problem so I'd get hold of them on site as it were. Sometimes I just used to pull them out of the wall at gateways.'

James winced.

'Yes I know it was terrible really. I didn't think at the time. It was a crusade, I had to outwit him in his...'

'Mass rabbiticide.'

'Cruelty to animals. Anyway one day I was pulling a nice stone from inside that hedge going along by the road to Tregarrow and there was some slow, noisy lorry on the road. Well, it passed, I saw it through a gateway but the noise was still there. And it was getting louder. I looked round and there was his tractor with him on top just glaring at me and coming up really fast! I ran. Only I couldn't because it was muddy. I was gripping the stone, stupidly, it was as if I thought I didn't even have time to throw it away. Then he started yelling something only I couldn't hear what and I looked round and he sounded a lot louder but he didn't seem that much closer, though he was closer, I knew that. I just kept running. Then I lost a boot.'

James understood. 'I can just see it. Which was most terrifying, being captured by the Ferocious Farmer or going home without your boot?'

'Ferocious Farmer indeed! It wasn't funny. You should have seen him. That dark evil face under the dark beret mouthing things at me.'

'So you abandoned the boot?'

'No, I grabbed it and carried it, nearly getting my leg stuck in the mud in the process. Left the stone though. Then I staggered along till I took off the other boot. There was a terrific roar and I looked round and all I could see were these huge wheels churning mud almost on top of me so I just dived into the hedge. I was sure he was going to kill me, squash me against the hedge or something. I climbed up the wall part, shoved the boots through and then struggled through the branches till I crashed through down onto the road. He went on roaring away in the field and I ran as fast as I could with lumps of mud for feet till I got home. Here, yes here, of course.' I looked round the room which seemed strange now.

'You must have looked very colourful. What did you tell them?'

'Oh, I was chased by a herd of bullocks. The thing is as I was running home, I knew I couldn't tell them the truth and I started not to believe it myself.' My voice was shaking, just telling it.

'But it didn't cure you, I'm sure. You went back at the dead of night with a trusty band of friends.'

'You bet it cured me! I got a dreadful cold and was off school for days, lying in bed and willing Mum's footsteps to come upstairs and what with that and the memory of his evil face scowling and glaring at me... well that was the end of *action direct* for me for a while, forever I think.'

James smiled but was only half attending. 'It's funny, you used the word "evil" about him twice. But he's not evil as such, is he? I mean he was only trying to live.'

'These things are hard to shift. I mean I still wouldn't go into The Duchy of Cornwall because of how whatsisname Trebilock refused you a drink that time. And for years I wouldn't talk to Carol Harris at school because our Dad and hers fell out over a mooring.'

'True. But. Well for a start I would never have called Trebilock evil. He died you know. The Duchy's all prettied up. Never go in there myself. Old Morgan – maybe his face looked distorted because you were scared.'

'Oh yes, and what was he shouting, "come 'ere my 'andsome. I got a nice little bird I rescued from a cat – would you like to look after it?"'

'I remember him being quite friendly that Christmas Day.'

'Yes, I remember him being very friendly too. It was extremely worrying. That was the same year and the months had gone by and he hadn't come and complained to Dad and then suddenly on the day of all days when you'd expect to be safe in the shelter of your family, the doorbell rings and – lo and behold;

Mr Morgan.'

'Our neighbour.'

*   *   *

As it turned out, James remembered quite a lot about Harry Morgan's Christmas visit. When the doorbell rang we had raced each other to the door. It might be someone interesting, bearing gifts. He stood there in the dark navy suit which, in a year or two would become tractor wear. His beret had been brushed. Seeing him not on his tractor was strange. He looked quite short. His dark face was creased and smiling as though smiling was all he ever did. My father, coming from the fireside, was so surprised that he hesitated before saying,

'Come in, Harry,' holding out his hand.

'Merry Christmas to one and all,' said Harry.

I fled. So did Penny. James stared and fidgeted and waited to see what would happen. In the kitchen my mother asked who it was.

'Mr Morgan.'

'Oh?' She undid her apron and stood there with her hands behind her back as if wondering whether or not to do it up again.

'I'll just go and see what he wants. You carry on.'

No more than three Brussels sprouts had passed through my trembling fingers before she was back, throwing her pinny

77

over her head, hurrying to the larder.

'Now I have to find room in the oven for mince pies for Mr Morgan. Here take this into the dining room.' She handed me a flat-sided bottle, labelled in my father's writing 'Sloe Gin 1958'. I looked at it and my mother.

'Can Penny take it?' This wasn't really a betrayal. She had immunity, I reckoned because of good behaviour.

'Go on. He won't bite.' I wondered if I could knock on the door. My father might answer it and then I could just hand him the bottle. But he called me in and then laughed at my shyness. Our visitor joined in. I hated it when grown-ups did that. And my father – whose side was he on? They were sitting in front of the fire. James stood by the Christmas tree at the window, pinging a bauble. Both men were smiling broadly.

'Wait till you try this, Harry. Sally, bring us the glasses.'

I took tumblers from the sideboard. James was staring at me. Forgetting it was Christmas Day, I gave him a quick, hard glare. They were the wrong glasses.

'We want liqueur glasses,' Dad said, sounding irritated.

'This'll do, this'll do,' said the farmer, cheery and accommodating. James came from the window to watch my father pour half a tumbler of sloe gin and hand it to his guest. He hesitated a moment before pouring the same amount for himself. James ran forward.

'Can I have some, Daddy?' This time they laughed at James.

'Go with your sister to the kitchen and get yourself some Corona,' said my father in a tone that suggested these were everyday delights.

In the kitchen my mother was pouring anthracite into a range stuck obstinately at LOW, its favoured position on Christmas Day.

'I'll just have to transfer the bird.' We hovered.

'Good idea, Mum!' said James, 'can I have a drink?'

'Yes, yes, help him, Sally. Where's Penny got to?'

Well out of the way, upstairs, I thought.

'Dunno.' I poured us some Dandelion and Burdock and returned to the vegetables. For a while things were quiet except for the occasional sigh from my mother. When I went back to the dining room with mince pies and the cook's request for a glass of sherry, Penny was sitting there. From her position on the floor in front of the fire, she gazed up at the two men. Her hair was nicely combed and she wore the new lemon yellow Orlon sweater her godmother had sent her. I marvelled at her courage. A few weeks after the event I had tried telling her about Meany Morgan chasing me on his tractor.

'You're making it up,' was all she would say.

Seeing him smiling at her so fond and friendly I knew she would never believe me now. My father stood up.

'All hands out of the kitchen!' I followed him to where my mother was riddling the stove.

'Let me do that, my darling,' he said, 'You go and talk to our guest – I'll pour you a nice drink. Off with the pinny!' He riddled with gusto. Smoke streamed from the stove. When he stood up he was flushed. With red, shiny faces they returned to the dining-room. I followed still carrying the mince pies. My father ushered my mother into his chair then stood leaning on the mantelpiece. James had returned to the window, hoping for snow.

'And Sultan?' Penny was asking, 'I never see him now. Did you put him out to grass?'

Why are you asking this, I wondered. We were quite certain he'd sent his horses to the knacker's yard.

'He went to my cousin over to Threemilestone, my lover.' It's a lie! I tried to catch her eye.

My mother raised her sherry glass. 'Happy Christmas, Mr Morgan.'

He drained his glass. My father lifted the bottle to him and he nodded.

Mother said, 'Is your sister spending Christmas with you, this year?'

'Same to you and many of 'em. Thank you, Michael. My sister is passing the day with me, yes.' He bowed his head. 'She sends you the compliments of the season, Ma'am.'

Mother gave a gracious smile. 'I suppose she's busy cooking the dinner?'

'Will you be having turkey?' asked Penny, her social style more advanced than her understanding.

He said nothing but leered towards her. A pause, then, 'Not turkey, no. Would anyone like to guess what I'm eating for my Christmas dinner?'

Penny puckered her brow.

'Can you guess, my 'andsome?' turning to me.

'Could it be … duck?'

'I know, I know,' James rushed triumphantly towards us, looked at his parents and shouted, 'Rabbit! Rabbit pie!'

My father gripped his glass, Mr Morgan paused before letting out a roar. Penny caught my eye and turned to the fire. Our mother was composed, hands in lap, glass between cool fingers. James looked to her for a response.

'I should think that would be very nice. Very nourishing and tasty. Good guess, James. But perhaps Miss Morgan is cooking… something… else for Christmas Day?'

We all waited for the roar to subside so he could tell us what he was planning to eat for Christmas dinner. But it subsided into a long self-perpetuating chuckle.

Eventually my mother asked, 'And will you both be listening to the Queen's Christmas broadcast this afternoon?'

'Will I, bugger 'ee! I won't be listening to no ruddy old queen. Bloody Duchy! What good did they ever do me? No thank you!'

At this my father's whole person changed. He had been looking down with an expression of reserved amusement. He was being hospitable, even expansive, but it was the public man. Now he took his arm off the mantelpiece and leaned back against it with a great grin on his face.

'Right Harry! Good man! What a system. What an absurd, nonsensical business!'

My mother rose to her feet. Penny and I followed. Penny said, 'But she's our young queen, isn't she Mr Morgan?'

'I must see how things are getting along in the kitchen,' said mother pleasantly, 'I have enjoyed your visit.'

'You wasn't offended I hope Missus.'

She said nothing. I saw her trying to catch my father's eye, then we left. James stayed for the show.

Back in the kitchen, Penny said, 'Puh! Something smells funny.'

'Oh my godfathers, the pudding's boiled dry!'

A hiss of steam and then the windows were opened onto

blue sky. What had happened to the Christmas Day walk? The turkey journeyed to and fro between ovens. Penny and I made breadcrumbs. We were friendly and giggly. Then she whispered 'Rabbit pie'. I was helpless. Mother told us it was rude to whisper and giggle like that so we said 'sorry' and were quiet until suddenly Penny turned to me, sticking out her front teeth and bulging her eyes, and set us going again.

It was after two o'clock by the time everything was ready. I had to fetch my father from the dining-room. He and Mr Morgan were both seated, leaning towards the hearth, no longer shouting. I heard my father mutter.

'And sent away to Australia just for stealing a rabbit.' I was told to stay and entertain Mr Morgan who immediately held out his glass. There wasn't much left in the bottle. I poured just enough not to finish it.

'It's a very nice drink,' he said and took a sip, smacking his lips together excessively. 'And you picked the sloes so I've been told.'

'Yes.'

He grabbed my wrist.

'And where'd 'ee get 'em to, they sloes?'

Not answering, I tried to pull my hand away, tried smiling.

'Where did the sloes come from?'

'A field, I can't remember.' At this point, James, who had been eating dates at the window, came over and said,

'I picked them. She didn't even come. I got all of them.'

By the time I left the room he was holding Mr Morgan's hand. In the kitchen my mother had rolled up a tea-towel like a charter, holding it with both hands.

'Well, I'm not Irish and I'm not a republican and I intend to listen to the Queen's Christmas Message.' My father looked from her glowing face to the kitchen table. The Crown Derby had been taken from a high shelf and the dust washed from every piece. It gleamed red, blue and gold. The meat dish was waiting with the serving dishes, their lids beside them. A tray held all the cutlery, including his carving knife and steel. In the background the turkey was a large hump on the stove.

'You have done a lot of work.'

She started to twist the scroll in her hands. He picked up the tray and led us into the dining-room.

'Will you join us, Mr Morgan?' my mother asked with good grace, having won. He wouldn't come to the table but ate from a plate on his knee. I wished he would go. I couldn't look at him and had to avoid Penny's eye. Just before pudding he fell asleep. His plate slid to the ground, taking with it a well gnawed bone. I don't remember him leaving, nor what the Queen had to tell the commonwealth that day.

James could remember him falling asleep – he had been reprimanded for laughing. He also recalled that much later, after Mr Morgan had finally left, Penny and I caused great merriment for him and both parents with our imitations of the Queen's voice.

'Old Morgan would probably have enjoyed it too,' James reflected, pushing a branch gently into the fire with the toe of his boot.

*　　　*　　　*

We were able to see our father alive just once more that melancholy October. It was hard trying to express the feelings to someone you had usually kept them from, especially when he could not even return the pressure of a hand. On our way out of the ward, James stopped to speak to Harry Morgan. He looked very different without his beret, his short hair all white now. The face had hardly changed and his black eyes shone like sloes. James made pleasant remarks; Harry took his hand.

'Is this here your wife?'

'No, this is Sally. You remember – my sister.'

He was amazed and stared at me as I stood there, grieving and bewildered. To James he said,

'She was a pretty one in those days. Two pretty girls. Lovely girls. There's been some changes, boy.'

When our father died, Penny came and arranged the funeral. She was quite certain about the things the Rector was a little unsure of. In the weeks that followed, James went back to the hospital several times to see Harry. I always had some reason not to go with him. Perhaps if Penny comes down, I thought, we could go together. Then to lunch, maybe, and I could ask really well-informed questions about the children. But she didn't come back. Harry just made it through to Christmas; he died before the New Year.

We went to his funeral, my mother and I and James, thinking that there would be few enough mourners. In fact there was a very respectable turn-out, about the same number as when our father was buried and mostly the same people.

THIS GAME

After a light supper of poached salmon and white wine the two men played chess. Father Feeny had refilled his curate's glass several times and matched him, glass for glass. Neither should be at a disadvantage. However, Gerry McCafferty was not giving the game his full attention. He wanted to be frivolous and the wine had made him bold enough to speak. He delivered his words with what he hoped was a roguish smile for he had no wish to offend the older man.

'Don't you sometimes wish you were a rabbi?'

The reply was immediate.

' "Were"? or "Had been"?'

'I mean…'

'So that you could be married and have children? Is that what you're saying?'

'Partly. Yes. And we could have women as colleagues.'

'Ah. Women priests. That's your notion, is it?'

Father Feeny was a man of great courtesy. Sometimes, though, a little scorn would show through, and this could make Gerry stumble in choosing his words. Now the wine no longer helped but was clouding his brain and the ideas which had seemed so sparkling felt puerile. The chessmen were waiting; Father Feeny's breathing was quiet and very steady. Gerry, who was playing black, looked at the board and fingered his queen's knight which was still on the back line.

Looking straight at him, his superior said, 'We have women colleagues, have we not? I have Mrs O'Neill. We work together in this house. I read. She dusts. I write. She cooks.'

Gerry's smile broadened. 'Ach, Father John, you know what I mean.'

'Not at all. I value Kathleen O'Neill as a fellow worker.'

Father Feeny returned to a scrutiny of the board. 'And what about the risen Christ?' he said, not expecting an answer. 'Come along, Gerry, what are you moving? We're playing Touch a Piece, Move a Piece, remember?'

It was not that Gerry had fantasies about eyes meeting across the sacristy, none of that Heloise and Abelard stuff, it was just that he longed for a companion, someone he could laugh with unchecked. And if a woman ever came as curate to Kilnalough, then she could take the Legion of Mary and he would have more time to coach the football team. It would have been nice to speculate about this even in an ironic way with Father Feeny. Now he pressed his finger into the carved black head of his knight. There was only one square free and it was covered by a white pawn, but move it he must and wait for the inevitable.

In fact it was only much later in the game that Gerry's knight joined all the other pieces taken by his opponent. The light they played in was rich and deep. Dark red curtains had been closed against the evening sun, and where these met only a blade of sunlight penetrated the room. It struck a framed print, one of a set showing the North Antrim coast. This one, glittering in the light, was well known to Gerry and always made him feel uneasy because it showed the Carrick-a-Rede Ropebridge. Without having to ask, he was sure Father Feeny had crossed over on it and that his nerve had never failed him because he had neither looked down nor pictured the sharp rocks and swirling waters below. Gerry could see him calmly walking on the swaying footpath over and back, over and back, just as many times as he felt like it.

Outside the room, beyond the curtains was the bay, with the town of Kilnalough beside it facing seawards to England.

The parochial house stood on a small headland. From the upstairs windows Father Feeny could have seen, had he wanted to, the comings and goings in the parish and, on the peninsula opposite, the new, rebuilt Imperial. Formerly a hotel, burnt down during the civil war, this building was already considered as Father Feeny's monument. Here the Operatic Society held their rehearsals, the Badminton Club met each week and the Football Team kept in training during the winter. People even remembered the Golf Committee meeting there before the new clubhouse was built. Father Feeny had been generously accommodating to the local Protestants, welcoming them not only into the new Imperial, but in a few cases into the Church itself. The lichen-covered grey building belonging to the Church of Ireland held services only once a month. Father Feeny found it more than suitable for recitals by the Renaissance Music Group.

Sounds of laughter and shouting from across the bay had been muffled all evening by the heavy curtains. These noises were dwindling now and the night breeze began to nudge at the window. Suddenly a piercing scream and wild harsh laughter came from across the water. Both men looked up. Father Feeny strode over and opened the curtains. The sea, all glimmering pallor, shocked with its sudden brightness. On the shore in front of the Imperial leaping figures were either fighting or dancing; it was hard to see which. Or were they embracing? Gradually the screams died into laughter and the laughter into something like the chatter of monkeys. The priests were unable to hear the words. They stood for a while at the open window. The air lifted away the room's familiar smell of polish and carpet, and the less usual smell of fish and wine, bringing in seaweed and dead crabs and car fumes.

In the distance the water was pale pink, like the inside of a shell. Gerry could see but not share its calm. He was worried that Father Feeny would ask him about the youngsters making the noise. He recognised the girls, one of them, Marcella Devlin, taller than the rest. She had been visibly fending off the even taller figure of Aidan Ryan, captain of the football team and Gerry's friend. But Father Feeny turned back to the room and did not enquire.

'Horseplay,' he said, switching on a lamp.

Perhaps the older priest was tired or affected by the break in concentration. He won the game only with great difficulty, Gerry having sustained what seemed like losses but turned out to be inspired sacrifices.

On these evenings of recreation it was their custom not to discuss parish matters. At ten o'clock they drank tea and ate the sandwiches left under a faded checked cloth by Mrs O'Neill. Then they watched the television news from London. Father

Feeny looked to England for his news, his culture and most of his friendships. Every morning after Mass he collected his paper, *The Daily Telegraph*, from the Ryans' corner shop. It was clearly marked as his, but once, as a child, Aidan had sold it to a summer visitor. Now in his twenties, Aidan claimed still to feel the shame of this. His mother had been in a terrible state. Would Father Feeny take *The Times* or *The Irish Times*? Aidan had rushed to help, seizing a copy of *Time* magazine, but Father Feeny had recoiled from the mere glimpse of its slippery bright cover. In the end the priest had patted him on the head and walked away with *The Farmer's Weekly*.

Gerry had enjoyed that story. Gradually he came to realize how misleading *The Daily Telegraph* was. A man for whom routine was ritual, Father Feeny was flexible, even liberal, over many parish matters. In Kilnalough there were girls serving at the altar and women were encouraged to share the readings and distribute communion. He spoke to Mrs O'Neill as he did to Gerry, politely, with dry, remote kindness. He must be nearly seventy and yet there was an elegance about him, a lightness. Despite his reserve, his movements at Mass were graceful. The ceremonies liberated something in him; he might have been a dancer.

Gerry felt clumsy beside him. Since his arrival as curate in Kilnalough three years earlier he had become rounder, especially in the belly.   Father Feeny might be a *bon viveur* but he was no Falstaff; Mrs O'Neill understood his tastes perfectly. Gerry, in the Curate's Residence, cared for himself.   A fry, tea and bread and jam were his evening meal.   His appreciation of homemade jam, carelessly uttered at a Bring-and-Buy sale, had resulted in so many offerings of this commodity that a press in the dining-room was bulging with jars all with handwritten labels showing the date of bottling.   These dates were slipping into the past and Gerry was failing to seize the day, while the press door became more and more difficult to close.   Then there were the daily presents of cakes and scones.   Aidan's mother was the worst.   Busy in the shop, she had no time to bake but would send Aidan over with buns and apple pies from the bread van.

Gerry was the one they spoiled.   To some of the women he was a pet, a darling.   He was so understanding.   When it came to comforting the bereaved it was Gerry they turned to. But it was Father Feeny they wanted to take the funeral.   And when it came to relationships, doubts about commitments or advice needed, the young people went to Gerry, but they still expected Father Feeny to perform the marriage ceremony.

For long stretches Gerry felt idle.   He did a lot of reading and meditating (staring into space) and drinking tea in the kitchen of the Curate's Residence.   He also took determined exercise.   In the early days he had walked on the beach between one headland and the next, but he was always aware that behind the palms which flourished there and the shrubs and wrought iron fences, curious eyes were watching his progress. So he went inland to the lough. He walked along the goat's path below the mountains, sat on the boulders and listened to the perpetual slapping of the small waves and told himself that most people were lonely in some way or another.

'Turn it off, Gerry.' This was not so much Father Feeny's comment on the TV news as an acknowledgement that Gerry would not want to know the sports results which followed. Instead he would go and watch *Match of the Day* at home. Father Feeny asked frequently to be reminded which team Gerry supported. He showed an amused interest only as long as it didn't have to extend to the names of the teams, the players, the managers or their positions in the league. He encouraged Gerry to work with the local team – 'Aidan Ryan's ruffians' he called them. Last year he had been very accommodating when it came to the Cup Final, letting Gerry off the vigil Mass on the Saturday. So it was a shock this evening when he said on the doorstep, 'I'd like you to come a little later and stay longer next week, Gerry. Something I want to talk to you about.'

Gerry walked back towards the town with the wind blowing in his face, muttering against his host in angry, un-clerical language.

'The old bastard must *know* it's the Cup Final next week! Is he teasing me or what? Is this some kind of a test?' He felt foolish as he thought of all the plans he had been making. A few Budweisers, frozen pizzas, a coal fire if the night got chill. Aidan would be watching the game with some of the crowd from the Imperial, but maybe they would feel like coming to him for the evening. Stupid! Fancy trying to behave like a normal person. What could the old man be wanting to talk about?

He pounded his way homeward without looking at the world around him. The wind domed his brow. He looked so wise but he raged inwardly at the coming deprivation. The tide was out and the street lights glimmered on wet sand.

*   *   *

'Gerry?' Aidan was on the phone next morning.

'Yes! Aidan.'

'Would it be a sin to take Marcella Devlin, tie a stone round her neck and drown her in the lough?'

'The lough, Aidan? Wouldn't the sea be handier?'

'Ah but the tides. She'd wash right in. The lough is deep, very deep in places.'

So far there'd been no laughter in Aidan's voice. Gerry tried to coax it now, laughing himself.

'Aidan, for the love of God, what has the poor girl done?'

95

Aidan had a way of dramatically lowering his voice several tones. 'She's trying to undermine the women's football team!'

'How *could* she do that?' It was Gerry's turn for mirthless irony.

'She just told them. Don't play.' He put on a high-pitched mincing voice. '"Football is not lady-like." No. "Football does not become a lady. It is *ugly* and *unfeminine*."'

'And did they listen?'

'Sure they listened. Two of them are making excuses already. I'll kill her. And the way she looked at me! Triumphant. Lips together, you know the sort of thing. Head in the air.'

'I thought you liked her. Could you not talk it over?'

Aidan growled. 'The only talking I'll do is, "You'd better go to Father Gerry McCafferty and make your last confession." So be prepared, Gerry, be prepared. Must go. Someone in the shop. See you later.'

Gerry had convinced himself that there was something seriously wrong with his priorities to have got so irrationally angry about a mere game of football. He put the matter well away from his mind as he concentrated on assisting Father Feeny at the eleven o'clock Mass. Aidan, too, looked no more murderous than usual and seemed indifferent to the presence of

Marcella just a few feet away.

This week Father Feeny spoke about vocations. In the last three years no one had come forward for the priesthood. Father Feeny did not mention this. He was not concerned to reproach. Nor did he stress sacrifice or talk of the deprivations of a priest's life. He spoke of joy and of need and he reminded the people of their great happiness. He spoke in the quiet, matter-of-fact tones he always used. There were few images, few examples. Just the words themselves, joy, privilege, gift, love. Bliss became familiar, heaven ordinary. From where he sat, Gerry could see Aidan's mother gazing at the altar with shining eyes.

When it came to the prayers, Gerry's were private and unorthodox. Recently, on the subject of vocations they had always been the same, that the Pope would allow discussion on the ordination of women, that those leaving who wanted to could be laicized so that his friend Micky could marry Anne and that, 'if it be Thy will', celibacy should no longer be a condition of the priesthood. He also had a mumbled hope, though this was not worded as a prayer, that any new priests sent as his fellow labourers should be normal and human, not freaks or paedophiles or anyone badly afflicted with body odour.

That evening, quite late, Aidan rang again. Gerry could hear women's voices in the background raggedly singing *I Will*

Survive as though they were trying it out for the first time. Aidan sounded cheerful and no longer intent on murder.

'Gerry. Saturday.'

'Oh God, Aidan, I forgot to tell you – I'm tied up.'

'How's that?'

'I have to see Father Feeny that evening.'

A pause.

'Why, does he not know? Tell him. See we're having a bit of a do. Molloys are getting a big screen and some of the lads are getting together and you're invited. It'll be great crack.'

'Sorry, Aidan. Sounds good, sounds great, but... Do not say anything to Father Feeny.'

'So will you not see the match at all?'

Gerry allowed himself a bitter comment, pretending it would sound like a joke, 'The only field I'll be at will be a black and white one.'

'Why? You've colour, haven't you, or Father Feeny has. Persuade him to watch it, not get Cut Off from the People kind of thing.'

'I mean we'll most likely be playing chess. Thanks for asking me. I'll speak to you soon.'

Less than five minutes later Aidan rang again. The 'survivors' in the background now sang in unison more or less and were thumping out the rhythm on the ground. Aidan had to shout.

'Gerry! Listen. Great idea! Guess what? I'll video it for you. You can watch it whenever you like.'

'Of course! Right! Good thinking, Aidan,' Gerry was beaming now. Why had he not thought of that?

'Charlie's idea. I'll get the tape. Just leave it all to me.'

'Well that really changes things. Thank you. Now we won't have to drag the lough for Father Feeny along with Marcella!'

There was a pause. *I Will Survive* came to an end. Gerry heard a wave breaking. Aidan said, 'I can't hear you.'

'Never mind. It was a joke.'

'Something about Marcella?'

'She's still alive is she, then?'

'Can you not hear her? That's her singing.'

Something like pride in his voice made Gerry ask, 'Is she forgiven?'

'Oh she's forgiven. She's just one crazy woman, that's all. Do you want to speak to her?'

'No. No for Heaven's sake. Good night, Aidan. Great idea about the video. See you later.'

On the morning of the Cup Final day, Gerry caught sight of Marcella walking past the Curate's Residence. She wore a flouncy skirt with big flowers, daises on a red ground, and, on top, a loose jumper with a high neck. The skirt might have been something her mother discarded along with *Heidi* and *Little Women* and the top could have come from anywhere, chosen with the sole purpose of disguising her shape. What brought the ensemble together was the vivid red lipstick which, even as far away as the garden gate, could be seen to match grotesquely the colour of her skirt. She glanced towards the front door, then looked at the ground, stopped, and retraced her steps. Gerry's hands were full of old newspapers; he was laying a fire for that night's viewing. When he looked up again she was still there. She had always had a strange way of walking, alternating long strides, hips swinging, with moments when she would stand utterly still. It reminded Gerry of the children's game where you move up on someone, then freeze at the moment they turn round. There were fewer pauses today and she was starting to brush her fingers on the top of the gate whenever she passed. She had the air of someone waiting for directions from above. Gerry muttered impatiently, 'Come on, Marcella. Touch a piece, move a piece, now.' He was afraid by the time he came back with the coal scuttle she'd be gone. He opened the front door at the same time as she opened the gate.

'I was coming to see you, Father.'

'Come in, Marcella. Nice to see you.'

He showed her into the sitting-room. 'Let me just go and wash *The Irish Times* from my hands. Like pitch it doth defile.'

She smiled remotely.

When he came back she seemed to fill the room. Declining to sit, she stood leaning against a table. From her clothes came strong perfume and a smell of cigarette smoke. Of course they all smoked at the Imperial. She shivered.

'Let me light the fire.' He had planned not to light it till the evening when he sat down to watch the match.

'No, no, not for me, Father.' She gazed at the Byzantine Madonna on the wall above Gerry's head. He slid sideways, like someone tactfully removing himself from someone else's photograph. He tried sitting in the fireside chair but from there she seemed too tall. He settled for a leaning position of his own, against the arm of the chair. Her foot started to tap. She arrested it immediately and took a packet of cigarettes from a pocket in her skirt.

'Will you permit me to smoke?'

'Permit? Surely, Marcella.'

He scrabbled in the sideboard for an ashtray. Embarrassed in case she caught sight of various unwanted treasures he had stashed away. But when he stood up, empty-handed, she was frowning at Rouault's *Head of Christ* over the mantelpiece. The intense, dark features seemed to displease her.

'I'll get an ashtray. You'll have a cup of coffee?'

'No, thank you, Father. What I have to say won't take long.'

She took the cigarette from the packet, put it to her lips, then waved her lighter at the Rouault.

'Forgive me for saying so, but I could never find that picture very *devotional*.'

What had happened to the girl's vocabulary? He was waiting for a suitable moment to remind her that she, like Aidan and most of the others, now called him Gerry. But 'Forgive me for saying so' and 'Permit me to smoke'? He hadn't remembered her smoking. Nor the pondering air of near menace she was emanating as if any moment she might snatch the pictures from the walls and outlaw all such comforts as coal fires and morning coffee. She had lit her cigarette and was staring at him as if challenging him to defend the painting. The defiance in her face suddenly reminded him of her fight with Aidan.

'So what was it you wanted to talk to me about, Marcella?'

She started to do her walk. From his place near the fire he saw her loom up, shoulders back, bright skirt swinging.

Then she paused, dropped her ash in the coal bucket, stared at the unlit fire and turned away again. At the other end of the room she sighed loudly and returned, keeping the same rhythm. This performance was repeated, her body's movements unvarying, only her face changing slightly, not in basic expression, which was a sort of determined blankness, but in where she bestowed her glance − on the Madonna, on the fireplace and then finally on Gerry. She stood in front of him, looked down, and said in the deepened tone which immediately brought Aidan to him, 'Gerry, you must pray for me.'

He took a moment to find his voice.

'Of course, Marcella. Of course. But tell me…'

A terrible thought came to him. She was pregnant. Not Aidan, please God, not Aidan.

She sank into the chair opposite him and bowed her head. When she turned to him again her face was radiant, her eyes suddenly magnified with tears. She controlled her red, trembling mouth.

'Ever since last Sunday.'

'Yes?'

'Well, Saturday night really.'

'Oh?'

'There was this picture in the paper. Little black children, Gerry, crying for food, orphans, nowhere to go. It was some kind of appeal for money and I thought, right, I'll do it, I'll give up the fags and I'll send the money to Trocaire every week that I would have spent on giving myself cancer.'

Now her manner was confidential and she was smiling indulgently as at some youthful foolishness. Gerry smiled back and nodded at the cigarette.

'So. When do you start?'

'But wait. Then on Sunday, Father Feeny preached about vocations. You remember?'

'Of course.'

'It was brilliant. And I started to think, why not? Why not me? And it was as if I heard a voice saying, not from outside, but inside, deep inside, "What is giving up a few lousy cigarettes compared to giving up your life?" And the feeling has grown, it just won't go away. Father, I have a vocation.'

Now she seemed amazed, exultant. She looked for his reaction. 'Is that how it was for you, Gerry?'

Relief and disbelief and a deep suppressed laughter. He must go very carefully. He needed something. A drink, but it would seem too early to celebrate. So a cup of coffee. He would have to insist.

'This sounds serious, Marcella. But you're not just planning to announce it and leave me. I'll put the kettle on.'

By the time he got to the kitchen his laughter was so

deeply buried he could scarcely manage a splutter. He was a little nervous as he filled the kettle and opened all the press doors before he remembered he was looking for an ashtray, thinking about Marcella. She was idle. She'd done nothing since leaving boarding-school three years ago. They'd put her in the Tourist Office for a while but she'd given a strange kind of welcome to the visitors. On one occasion, in an incident which produced open shock and secret admiration among the population of Kilnalough, she had responded to a request for directions to the Holy Well by making every member of the party remove socks and shoes and set out barefoot. Women in cotton dresses had been seen clutching each other and giggling, hopping from foot to foot as they unstrapped their sandals. The men looked awkward but they, too, obeyed. 'It's the custom,' she told them, so the story went, explaining to the locals that 'Customs have to start somewhere.'

When he returned with a tray, she was sitting in a chair with her eyes closed. Her cigarette end was in the hearth as were the empty packet and the cellophane wrapper of a new one. She seemed so unaware of her powerful and troubling sexuality that she might give that up without a qualm. But her smoking and her untidiness and her appetite for drama? He thought she had fallen asleep, but on hearing cup on saucer she was quickly on her feet.

'Stay where you are,' said Gerry, but she pulled out a seat and sat at the table.

Now he took her seriously. Listened to her, acted the devil's advocate, told her of the hardships of religious life. She had been taught by nuns. Did she really see herself living among them?

'But I want to go to Africa, Father, to work in the places where all the misery is and *do* something. There'll not be time for tensions and pettiness out there.'

He knew himself well and deeply, deeply enough to recognize that he was attracted by the idea of a celibate Marcella thousands of miles away from Kilnalough. Therefore he made his arguments stronger, mocked her and teased her, spoke of her family and then, just as she was rising to go, said, 'Are you sure you're not just running away from Aidan Ryan and the Ladies Football Team?'

She frowned and deepened her voice again. 'I'll not be sorry to say goodbye to the Imperial, no harm to Father Feeny.'

'Am I to say anything to Father about your...?'

'Would you? Please. I've felt shy about speaking to him myself. But I'd like him to know. It was he who inspired me.'

He walked to the gate with her. She seemed more confident now and more natural, but she did hold out her hand

and say with emphatic warmth, 'Thank you, Gerry. Thank you for listening to me. You will pray for me, won't you?'

*   *   *

'In the end I thought she was sincere. It's just that rather odd manner of hers...'

'Play-acting!'

Father Feeny was entirely dismissive of the good news Gerry had brought him. In truth neither of them really wanted to discuss it. The windows opened onto a gentle evening and the sun had yet to sink behind the mountain. Its light deepened the blue water of the bay, making it look solid enough to walk on. Molloy's Bar, 'The Water's Edge', had its window open too and every so often spilled out gasps and broken cheers like hiccups.

Mrs O'Neill had spread them a more sumptuous meal than usual. Gerry noticed an ice-bucket with a fat bottle resting in it. He also saw that the shining polished wood of the chess-board was empty and the box closed at its side. He was drawn to the dining table with its winking glasses and cutlery, and his pride at the news about Marcella was fast dissipating. He was also curious as to what Father Feeny wanted to tell him; it had better be big enough to miss the match for. But reconciled about the match, he was beginning to enjoy this evening. Only he owed it to Marcella to argue for her, to affirm her seriousness.

Surely Father Feeny would be glad to know of the effectiveness of his preaching.

'Perhaps I should suggest she speaks to you herself?'

'Yes, perhaps you should. Now. A glass before we dine?'

It really was champagne. Father Feeny opened it with such decorum and neatness of aim that Gerry was struck by the contrast with recent news images of sports heroes spurting triumphant froth into the crowd. What was he brought here to celebrate? Last month for his fortieth anniversary as a priest the whole parish had made a fuss of Father Feeny and he had tolerated it with good humour, clearly glad when it was over.

They stood with their glasses at the window. Gerry wanted to say 'This is the life!' ironically but the irony would have seemed like bad manners. Outside the beach was empty and the waves too gentle to hear. An angry roar burst from 'The Water's Edge'. Maybe later he would guess from the video what that was about.

A breeze rattled the window on its catch and Father Feeny, handing his glass to Gerry, stopped to close it. His movements seemed slower and Gerry was aware of the will behind his straightening up again. He took back his glass and led the way to the fireside.

'What I have to tell you won't take long but you may

want to ask me some questions and that would seem reasonable. Perhaps you'd care to replenish our glasses.'

As Gerry poured the wine he heard distant sounds of life from the beach, callings and laughter which just came through the closed windows. 'Half-time,' he said to himself and reflected that this was the second time today that someone had promised not to take too long.

Father Feeny selected a damp piece of worm-eaten driftwood from the creel and threw it in the fire where it hissed and sparked. There was something unusually offhand about his gesture. Gerry sat perched opposite, expectant, politely smiling.

'Well, Gerry, I've been at this game for over forty years now.'

His voice sounded strangely rough-edges, like a hard man in the movies.

'It's a great achievement!'

'Yes, I think so. I've done some good things. And now I'm going to chuck it in.'

He looked straight at Gerry and waited.

'You're going to retire?'

'Yes, I'm going to retire.'

Gerry raised his glass uncertainly.

'Well. Congratulations.'

'I'm not sure that you understand. I'm retiring, yes. But I'm also, as we used to say, dropping out.'

'You're saying that you...'

He hoped that Father Feeny would complete the sentence but he just sat there, apparently relaxed, in his black suit, only betraying the slightest unease by the tightening of his fingers on the glass.

'You're retiring as a priest?'

'Yes. I shall become a lay person. I shall no longer say Mass or hear confessions, or bury people or marry people or baptize their children.'

Gerry was so unable to believe this that he again thought he was being tested.

'But surely you could retire, you've earned it I'm sure, and not do those things and still be a priest, still say Mass.'

'I knew you would be shocked, Gerry.' He gave the first smile of the whole encounter. 'I'm expecting a lot of people will.'

Gerry was more than shocked. He couldn't meet Father Feeny's look. He stared at his glass, at the fire, at Father Feeny's well polished shoes on the rug in front of him. There was a long silence. Gerry tried to think of something to say.

'Come to the table now,' the old man said, 'and you can ask me if there's anything you don't understand.' The throwaway tone had gone now and he sounded kind and patient and a little tired. As he shared out cold roast meats and ham, pickles and salad and bread, Father Feeny outlined his plans. He would rent a house in Ballycastle where his sister and a niece were living. A house-keeper would be found for him and the proprietor of the Royal Hotel was an excellent cook. 'I think I shall be able to persuade him to do me Meals on Wheels.' He smiled. 'I shall walk on the beach. I may get a dog – I like dogs – there's a music society and it's within reach of Belfast which, as you know, I much prefer to Dublin. And, as I know you're wondering, yes, I shall go to Mass, perhaps not every day. It'll be such a relief to have someone else do the hocus pocus.'

Gerry nodded stupidly. He couldn't respond properly. It seemed he was always to feel confused here among the neatly hung prints and the chess pieces and to be clutching a wine glass, at a loss for words. He tried to warm to Father Feeny's plans but in most of his mind there was outrage. This was desertion – and with a smile! There had to be something behind it. Even so late in life it could happen. *Cherchez la femme!*

'Have you told Mrs O'Neill?'

'No. Apart from my sister you are the first. I shall miss Mrs O'Neill.'

'And she'll miss you. We all will.'

'Kind of you to say it. But I would have to be going

sooner or later. I'd rather not wait for you-know-who to shuffle the cards once more.' He inclined his head towards the place where the bishop lived.

And then the jokes began. References to the bishop (You-know-who, His nibs, Himself) had been wry and allusive in the past. Now the jokes came like birds gathering in the branches. Gerry found it hard to concentrate. Somehow Marcella was back in the conversation. 'What about it then, Gerry? Twenty, thirty years' time and it's Marcella for bishop. Wouldn't she make a good one? I can see her in the vestments now.'

Gerry joined in but his laughter was shaky. This was more than he could handle. He thought of Micky Martin twenty years ago in that cold room in Portknock trying to weigh his love of God and his desire for Annie McCallion. Or was it the other way round? 'Do I know what love means?' he had asked Gerry, who sat frowning, trying to identify.

And now here was the champion, the man who took all prizes for integrity and commitment, raising his glass to 'Marcella for bishop, Marcella for Pope!'

Gerry felt ashamed that he had laughed at Marcella. He would talk to her again. But what would he advise her now?

He tried to return to stable things, asking Father Feeny some practical questions which were easily answered. He dealt so blandly with it all that Gerry realized this had been planned for a long time. Gerry lacked the courage or their friendship lacked the intimacy for him to ask Why? Only towards the end of the evening did the parish priest come close to explaining.

'I don't believe it's His will that an old man should rise early on cold mornings to perform a service for a few other freezing souls when the job can perfectly well be done by somebody else. I've played my part and played it to the best of my abilities. It's you turn now, Gerry. Or perhaps the Marcella Devlins of the world.'

Gerry walked home in a state of bitter confusion. The town was quiet now and the lights reflected on the bay came and went as breezes ruffled the water. His anger of a week ago had been specific, pure even, compared with what he felt now. It was like trying to walk on very dry sand. When Micky left it had been to get married. Others had political reasons. But Father Feeny had no need. The worst of it was the feeling that the old man's decision exposed his own conservatism. He was a plodder, worthy, unimaginative. There was something quietly, infuriatingly radical in Father Feeny's action.

The phone was ringing as he opened the front door.

'Yes, Aidan. Yes, I've just kicked against it coming in the door. No, not jogging, just coming in. No, you're right, don't tell me the score. Good, good, I'm glad you enjoyed it.

No, DON'T TELL ME! I'm looking forward to it. I'll be watching it now. Enjoy your evening. Yes. Thank you, thank you. Goodbye.'

He set up the video and brought a can of Budweiser and a packet of crisps from the kitchen. The small lamp near the TV blew its bulb as he switched it on. He sat in the darkness staring at the bright screen. He had to stay. It was an act of duty, of love even. The game seemed like a good game, full of incident. He remembered the cries from the shore, the howls of near agony which had been the background to Father Feeny's untroubled revelations. Something Aidan said had led Gerry to expect a result of one-all, but he sat there with a headache deepening in his skull, it gradually became clear that this was to be a goalless draw.

AT MISS MULLIGAN'S

It was in the summer, the year Buddy Holly died. Elvis, of course, was still alive, but neither of them was listed on the juke box in Molloy's Bar in Glentubbrid. I was wondering what to choose and if I dare play it, the place was so quiet. My mother sat up at the bar with her gin-and-orange, smoking, talking in a murmur to the barman. My father, as usual, had established friendliness with smiles and little laughs and was now coming to help me choose. Nodding towards my orange juice, he whispered, 'Would you rather have a Babycham?' But I was just growing out of Babycham and I said 'No thanks' because I wanted him to stay with me at the juke box and not go joking with the barman or pretending to defy my mother over me drinking alcohol at the age of fifteen.

I hadn't heard of most of the names on the juke box. In the end he chose Ruby Murray, *When Irish Eyes are Smiling*. My mother turned round and made a face. I asked if I could have something to eat because I was starving and she said 'Wait.'

We had come a long way from England for this holiday, a long journey by road and boat and road again. I looked out at the view from the bar window. I could see mountains and ordinary looking fields and grey clouds. This was my mother's country. I had heard so much about Donegal. When we arrived I had expected her to kiss the ground or take great draughts of the wonderful Irish air but she made straight for the bar where she now seemed at home.

When the music stopped she asked the barman, 'Johnny, who's doing Bed and Breakfast now? Is Miss Mulligan still going?'

'She is, surely. There's one or two staying there now but I'm sure she'd fit you in.'

We drove a couple of miles. It was beginning to get dark. Miss Mulligan's was a tall house standing a little way from a cluster of much smaller ones. There was a car parked outside, a large one, facing outwards. It was the windows of the house that were tall, two on either side of the front door.

When the door opened, the fading light shone on a face as white as a mask. My mother said, 'Miss Mulligan, you may remember...'

There was no pretence. 'Come in Patricia Sweeney. Johnny said you'd be coming. And this is your husband. And your daughter.'

She wore a vivid red blouse tucked into a very full black skirt. We followed her through a dark hall towards a lighted room and closer all the time to the smell of food.

There was one table already occupied by a middle-aged couple, eating from full plates. The man nodded briefly, a little crossly I thought, as though we were intruding. The woman smiled extravagantly.

We sat near them. The rest of the room was dim and veiled in smoke from the kitchen. I was so hungry I could not join my father in his game with the place mats. He picked up his and peered at it then at mine and my mother's.

'I'll swap the Carrick-a-Rede Rope Bridge for Derry's Guildhall or Mount Errigal.' He said it loud enough to be heard at the other table but the smiling woman was busy pouring tea.

'Behave yourself, Robert,' my mother said, but now she too was smiling, happy to have arrived.

In the centre of the table were ketchup, vinegar, salt and pepper and an ash-tray. My mother had already slid this towards her. There should be a menu, I thought.

A large tea-pot arrived and a plate of bread and butter. I was well through the bread by the time our meal arrived. Even at that stage in the fifties, post-war austerity lingered in England. We were respectably silent at the sight and smell of sausages, liver, bacon, eggs and potato bread.

My mother finished the meal in her usual way, with a sigh and a cigarette. My father got up and examined the pictures on the walls and nodded and smiled at the other couple.

My mother asked me in a kind voice if I had enjoyed the food and I said I did and asked her the same. I felt too heavy to follow my father in his tour but I could see that there were two pictures, old-fashioned looking, one of a couple saying their prayers in a field, the other of workers gathering corn. There were also painted wooden plates of a flamenco dancer and a bull fighter, and on the further wall, too dim for me to see properly, what looked like framed cut-outs from newspapers. Behind me, a straw donkey and a shawl had been pinned up, looking as though they had come down and been put up again and might come down again soon.

Leaning slightly I could see into the kitchen. Miss Mulligan had a helper, a girl a bit younger than me. My father drifted to the door and spoke to her and I suppose he said something nice because the young girl looked a bit confused, but pleased. I thought she blushed but it was hard to see. It gave me a feeling I didn't much like. It was funny that my mother never minded him praising other people but I did.

Just as we were leaving the dining-room a woman came in by herself. She looked weary as if the day had been too much for her.

'I'm sorry I'm late, Josie. Tomas is just coming.'

Josie, so that was her name. Josephine Mulligan. Whoever Thomas was he did not appear. It was funny the way she stressed the second syllable of his name.

Miss Mulligan showed us to our room. There was a big, high double bed with a huge eiderdown and then at the foot of this a small folding bed 'for the wee girl'. Me!

She turned her attention to me. 'You'll be grand here,' and she fussed a little with the cover of my bed which was also an eiderdown reaching to the floor on both sides. She had a friendly smell of the kitchen. I noticed how quickly the colour came and went from her face and I tried to penetrate her smile which was frequent but not warm. I knew my mother approved of such business-like people while my father would try to woo them. I just said 'Thank you' and wondered how long we would be staying.

Later, as I was falling asleep I heard my mother talking about her in bed.

'The black hair is new. She was blonde, well a sort of strawberry blonde the last time I saw her. Oh years ago, you know, when I came over for Daddy's funeral.'

'Nice place,' murmured my father, from the comfort of the big bed.

2

Next morning, early, I woke to hear my father tip-toeing from the room. He was dressed. It was too early for breakfast, though the crows and seagulls were about. The heavy curtains let in blades of light at the sides. It seemed to be sunny, but I wanted more sleep.

Last night I had slept at once, but now the narrow bed was ejecting me with its hard frame pressing through the mattress. When I was sure my father wasn't coming back soon, I climbed into the big bed beside my mother. She opened her eyes and looked at me and murmured something, then turned away. Her back was bony. It always had been. The pillow was quite lumpy where my father had stuffed his pyjamas under it. Apart from that it was cosy and warm. Soon my mother started snoring and I drifted off. Then I woke to her saying, 'Ellie, don't kick! Lump!' so I moved right to the edge and went back to sleep.

I woke to opened curtains and cigarette smoke. She was sitting up beside me with a cup of tea and a cigarette burning in the ash-tray. My father was back, perched on the side of the folding bed.

'Watch that, Robert,' said my mother, 'it'll tip up.'

'So Goldilocks is awake at last,' he said.

I scowled, though he didn't need to explain, 'So you found our bed "just right".'

'Close the door, Robert,' said my mother, 'I can smell breakfast.'

It smelled like last night but with more bacon to it and a background note of burning toast.

'How long are we staying here?' I asked.

He passed this on to her with a look and she just said, 'We'll see.'

At breakfast we sat at the same table. Miss Mulligan was wearing the same black skirt, this time with a yellow blouse. She clicked about the dining-room. When the door to the kitchen opened I saw the young girl carrying plates. Following my glance, my father said, 'That's Mary. She lives in the village. You could get to know her. She might show you round on her day off.'

I made a polite noise in response but I hoped he would forget this idea. I found it hard enough to talk to people I knew, but a stranger, no. Also I'd seen the village last night and there wasn't much to see.

He continued to share, in a low murmur, the information he had gathered on his morning outing: Mary had left school and was Miss Mulligan's only helper. She walked to and from home, two miles. Miss Mulligan had no car. That couple who

121

were at the next table last night were Mr and Mrs Andrews from Lisburn near Belfast. They went to a different place of interest every day. This was their first visit to Donegal. The butcher's van came twice a week and so did the van from Jimmy's, the village shop. My mother remembered Jimmy and his van. Could it possibly be the same van, she wondered.

Mr and Mrs Andrews came in and sat down. He wore a bright yellow cravat spotted with some tiny objects I couldn't see properly. Vintage cars, perhaps. His wife was huddling under her white cardigan.

I buttered my toast and stared out of the window at a lumpy wall and some dark-leaved trees. Through the leaves moving in the wind, I could see a field but no sheep or cows. The early sunshine had gone and the sky was darkening. Mr Andrews asked, 'Could we have some light please?' and peered at his plate, in a mime of visual deprivation. When Miss Mulligan switched on the light with a smile, it made very little difference, but Mrs Andrews thanked her warmly. It was agreed between our two tables that it would soon be raining.

When it came, the rain hit the windows. Trees and field were blotted out. It was different from rain at home; it was like Devon or Brittany rain. Holiday rain.

The quiet lady from last night came in with a boy who must be her son. So this was Thomas. I couldn't see his face properly. He was tall and skinny, gangly even. A bit older than me, probably. When they sat down he had his back to us. I could see that he had dark hair and a thin neck. I only glanced at him. I didn't want my father to be getting ideas. Besides I was being faithful to Julian.

It was still raining after breakfast. 'What is there to do?' I asked, irritating my mother.

'Come for a spin with me,' my father said.

'Where? Round graveyards?'

He was on a quest to find the Irish roots he was sure he had. His mother was Jane Dunne. He was sure he would find her family name on some stone, something that would tell their story, if only a date or the name of a place. My mother was tolerant, even kind about this. She had no need to search; she knew who she was and where she came from.

Looking round graveyards in the rain was not my idea of a holiday so I said, 'Not today, thanks,' and he went off, saying he was sure it would brighten up later.

3

My mother and I crossed the landing from our room to the sitting-room. It was large and dark and although there were two windows, heavy curtains blocked off much of the light. You could see more fields and trees. She said, 'You should be able to see the bay from here when it stops raining.'

She pointed out a bookcase. 'This would be a nice quiet place to read, look,' gesturing to the sofa and armchairs. Then she left me, saying she was going to borrow Miss Mulligan's iron.

The bookcase was of solid wood and dusty. It was constructed like a classical doorway with scrolled columns on either side. The books were all old and battered, even the hardbacks. There were children's books with strange coloured pictures in shades of emerald green and cherry red, guidebooks with dreary black-and-white photos and also a shelf of paperbacks. These all seemed to have different people's names written inside the front cover, guests, I supposed, Jessica Partridge and J. O'Sullivan. And there were those green Penguins which my friend Bunnie and I used to read, Agatha Christie, Dorothy L.Sayers, Josephine Tey. My hopes lifted at the sight of a colourful-looking Georgette Heyer but I'd read it before. Someone had almost completed I-Spy at the Seaside.

Across the room a sideboard turned out to be a radiogram. Its cupboards which I thought were locked were only stiff and opened with a tug. Out came haphazardly piled records, some 78s, some LPs and singles. I looked for something to play but I didn't know any of them except a 78 of John McCormack. My father loved him but I could never see why. A lot of the rest seemed to be Latin-American dance music. And there was someone called Jean Sablon singing *Two Sleepy People*. I sensed something homely about it all as if it had meant a lot to some people, a family perhaps, but I felt outside it and didn't think I could even try to play these records.

I stood at the window, pulling the curtains open wider. Dust floated gently from them. The rain was steady. A blue van had arrived outside; there was rain jumping off its roof. I saw Mr and Mrs Andrews setting out in their big car, making spray from the puddles. There was no sign of the sea, not even fields, just the hedge on the other side of the road. Somehow the dust and gloom made the room seem safe and protecting, as if life with its hazards went on elsewhere.

I took a green detective story, *The Franchise Affair*, and settled in one of the armchairs. I felt tired and heavy. It wasn't just the huge breakfast, it was a sleepiness I recognised, a-day-in-the-summer-holidays sleepiness.

I curled up in the chair; it was very comfortable. It had an old smell, like the floor of a deep forest, a smell like dead leaves and fungi.

I slept for a while and heard voices in the road outside. I looked out and it was still raining but the boy was out there with a bike. A passer-by, also on a bike, was shouting something at him. Then the boy rode off.

'He'll get soaked.' I thought, secure in the big room.

Miss Mulligan came in.

'Are you all right in there? You've plenty to read anyway. Your mammy tells me you're a great reader.' She looked round. 'You need a light. I'd be afraid of you damaging your eyes. Stay where you are.'

I stayed. Where would I go? She went out but knowing she was coming back I sat on the edge of the chair and looked at the pattern on the carpet – dull red and blue flowers inside boxes inside boxes – and wondered if I could ask where my mother was. It was quiet and I could hear the rain and the distant, muffled noises of the house, voices and kitchen sounds. I began to feel sleepy again.

She came back at last, awkwardly dragging a standard lamp. 'I think this works. Where are you sitting?'

The lamp had a long wriggly flex. She positioned it behind my chair and 'There – it works!' and she stood back in wonder.

'It's very nice,' I said, genuinely admiring its yellow silk shade and the glow coming from it.

'There you are. That'll save your eyes. I'll tell your mother.'

'Where is she?'

'Having a cup of tea. Will you take a cup?'

'Yes please.' I began to pull myself up from the chair.

'No, stay where you are. It'll be brought.'

She seemed cheered by the success of the lamp, her smile had a natural gaiety about it. And yet I still felt unsure of her. Did she like me? Perhaps it didn't matter, but to me it did.

I was settled back with the book under the lamp when the girl, Mary came in with the tray.

'Now where will I put this? No – stay where you are.'

She put the tray on the sofa and found a small table which she placed beside me, as pleased with this arrangement as Miss Mulligan had been about the lamp. On the sofa the tea had spilled over into the saucer. Mary poured it back into the cup. She looked at me nervously but then we both giggled. There was a plate of bread and jam with butter spread in thick wedges.

'Your Mammy's in the kitchen. I was talking to her. She's very nice.'

'Yes, I suppose she is. I mean, yes, very.'

People were always telling me how nice my mother was, like my schoolfriends when they came to stay. Bunnie loved her. I got the impression she was popular in the staff-room at Woodbury High School for Girls where she was the French teacher.

Mary was looking at the top of my head. 'Your hair looks beautiful under the lamp. It brings it out lovely. Really golden.'

I was ungracious of course. 'It's just mousy.   It's messy.'

'Oh no, it's lovely.   Not like mines.   Do you like reading?'

'Pretty much.   Do you?'

'Oh I love it.   Women's magazines and *Ireland's Own* and *The Far East*.   I like true stories.   Not them sort of books,' nodding towards *The Franchise Affair*, 'I wouldn't be bothered with nothing like that.   Tomas would be a great reader.'

'Thomas?'

'You know, he's staying here.   He's my cousin.'   She went pink and looked at the tea-tray. 'Well I'd best be going.'

Just before she reached the door she turned and said without smiling 'See you later, alligator.'

'After a while, crocodile.'   I replied.

In spite of Mary's efforts, drips from the bottom of the tea-cup fell onto the open page.   I sort of smeared it in and read on.   I was already a bit disappointed with this book.   It turned out that the 'Franchise ' was the name of a house not a person and I was starting to realise that 'affair' was not what I had hoped.

The rain continued.   I went to the window.   There was no-one about, no cars in front of the house, just puddles with the rain hitting them.   I noticed a green post-box in the wall at the side.   That would be handy if we were staying much longer.   I could write to Bunnie.   Not that anything had happened.

Everything was ordinary really, just a different kind of ordinary.

My mother came to tell me we were having lunch here today. She was wearing her new candy-striped shirt-waister. It was dark pink and white. She looked clean and nice and made me feel how grubby I was and my hair needed brushing. I'd spent too long curled up in the big chair.

'What's for lunch?'

'Soup. Go and wash your hands and brush your hair.'

I didn't have the energy to glare at her for talking to me in the wrong tone.

Wet leaves brushed the bathroom window. Their deep green was soft against the bright acid green of the painted walls. It was a funny-shaped room, partitioned out of our bedroom, I worked out, with a very high ceiling. There was a bath and a blue shower-curtain decorated with shells and sea-horses. I knew other guests shared it with us – I'd heard a man clearing his throat there before breakfast – but no-one had left towels or toothbrushes. There was just some bright pink soap in the basin. I washed with that. It was nice, like the cheap kind I gave Bunnie at Christmas. It woke me up a bit.

We ate in the kitchen. Chairs scraped the tiled floor. The soup was watery and cabbage-y. I hesitated, but my mother glanced at me so I ate it. There was plenty of the good bread. It was called wheaten bread and we praised it.

The range was lit; it made the room very hot. Above our heads the flies fastened themselves to a long, crowded fly-paper. They were coming in through the open window. Looking out I could see steps leading up to the garden and the sycamore branches swaying. There were swallows dashing about, criss-crossing the yard. I always wished I could be like them.

Miss Mulligan was now wearing a thin black nylon blouse and I could see her bra through it. This was a little embarrassing like when a teacher dressed that way sometimes at school. Tarty, I thought.

'Where's Dad?'

'He'll be gone all day.'

'He'll be getting wet.'

'I expect he'll shelter in the car.'

Only Mary and Miss Mulligan were there, but I felt that our conversation was being held in front of an audience.

I went back to my chair and my book. When I felt sleepy I made myself trawl the room for something to look at. The pictures on the walls were landscapes. They had a far-off quality as though they had been spectacular once upon a time. I thought the mists of time had dulled them. Yellow grasses and gleams of light and cattle long-since dead. The descendants of these cows were not painted, I was sure, the way we and our ancestors were. But then there were sometimes people in the fields performing various agricultural tasks and what did we know about them and their families? Perhaps they had eaten the cattle.

I needed someone to talk to! Apart from Mary and Miss Mulligan and my mother all talking about practicalities, I hadn't exchanged a word with anyone. My father would have joined in my thoughts about the cows under the trees. I wondered if Tomas would talk about such things. Mary had said he was a great reader.

There was one picture which involved a bull but it was very very different. This was painted on a wooden plate in thick bright colours. It showed a bull with its head down looking murderous while from behind, a bull-fighter in bright red with arms raised was about to plunge long darts into its shoulders. I reached to touch it and could feel the thickness of the paint. Some dust came away on my fingers.

I moved quickly past a framed certificate. It was in Irish and the name may have been Miss Mulligan's. My mother claimed to have forgotten the Irish she learned at school but she might know. I was more interested in why Miss Mulligan had a bullfighter on her wall.

How old was she? I wondered. Sometimes she looked far older than my mother but she dressed in a sort of in-between way, only Bunnie and I would never dress like her nor would our mothers. I couldn't pick out what it was. Was it the hair? Or the high-heels? Or the tight-waisted skirts as she brushed past our tables?

In the mirror my pale face loomed out of the twilight. It looked interesting. I pulled back my hair and turned to the side, and tilted my face to show my cheekbones. Yes, I did look a little like Juliette Greco. Julian had said that. I knew he thought I was attractive, although he never said so. Other, more handsome men would adore me one day. But would any man dance as well as him or know such good jokes?

In my head I started a letter to Bunnie. But I began to read and drowsed again and suddenly my father was covering me with an eiderdown. I sat up.

'Where have you been?'

'Go back to sleep, Goldilocks, I'll tell you later.'

But I had done enough sleeping. 'Where did you go?' I asked. He said he had been driving around and he'd found a graveyard where the Protestants let the Catholics bury their dead in the old days. Or was it the other way round? I had only ever half-listened to him.

'So you see their bones lie together quite happily,' he said, and I remembered that.

'Can we go somewhere now?' I asked.

'Poor lamb. Are you feeling a bit cooped up?'

4

The rain had stopped. We went to the sea, just me and him. The sea was flat and pale and so was the sky; you couldn't see where they joined. It was a wide shore, a long pale beach with one breaking wave the whole length of it. We stayed at one end, skidding about on the rocks. My father tied to pop the bubbles on bladder-wrack but he was hopeless at it and I had to show him how.

As we drove back we saw the boy from Miss Mulligan's, Tomas, cycling to the beach. He was riding down-hill, leaning forward over the handle-bars. My father waved at him but the boy couldn't take his eyes off the road. It was strange that I'd never seen his face, just the back of his head at breakfast and now the top of it. In both places his body had seemed tense and serious.

'I used to love going to the shore,' my mother said at dinner. 'We walked there of course.'

'It was wonderful!' my father said,

'I want to talk to you after,' she told me.

I hadn't done anything. I hadn't had a chance and Bunnie wasn't there and there were no boys. Not in a real way anyhow.

After dinner she led me to the sitting-room. It was empty.

'This room isn't really used,' she said. 'Would you like to sleep here? I've spoken to Miss Mulligan.'

'Um... I don't know...Yes all right.'

It would be better than sharing with them. A whole big room to myself. But ...

'Are you sure no-one will want to come in? There're books and records.'

'No, you can just close the door. People watch television in The Back Room or stay in their rooms. So. We'll bring in your bed shall we?'

This was the first I'd heard of a television. The bed came in, but I knew I would sleep on the sofa. I could use the lamp for reading in bed. My father brought in my bedding and sat talking for a while. He wanted to be sure I was happy about the move. I showed him the books. He borrowed *The Daughter of Time* and said I was the librarian and he hoped I'd let him off for not bringing his card.

When I was alone I looked out at my view. The rain was back and the puddles in the road were getting bigger. No-one passed. The Andrews' car and ours were side-by-side in the layby. Theirs was pointing outwards.

I surveyed my room. Some changes could be made. It was very over-furnished but I might find a way to move things about a bit and make some spaces. And if I put an upright chair at the sideboard I could use it as a writing-place and do my letters and cards there. Or perhaps it would be better to use the low table next to an armchair.

I folded up the folding bed and placed it against the wall. Then I made up my bed with sheets, pillow and blanket on the sofa. I put on the golden yellow standard lamp and snuggled down in my clothes. I would wash and change in the bathroom later. Meanwhile I lay there making plans. Even if it rained I had to go for walks – I was feeling the weight of Miss Mulligan's dinners. I would listen to my mother's memories of this place and ask Mary about her life. I might even go with my father on one of his graveyard jaunts. Also I would find a way to say 'hello' to Tomas.

5

My father took me to the beach again the next day on his way to whatever graveyard quest he was planning. He would pick me up later, he said. I was happy enough because the sun was shining at last. I had my towel and swimming things and a book to read. My mother had asked Miss Mulligan for sandwiches for me. Mary made them and handed them to me with a sympathetic smile.

'It's boring at the shore. What'll you do all day?'

I thought she must be covering up her envy, poor Mary,

working away in that hot kitchen.

After an hour or so at the beach I began to have an idea what she meant. I found a dry sandy place above the tide line and spread out my towel. I had on my new swimsuit under my clothes. It was my first-ever bikini. The top was under-wired and pushed up my breasts in a way I thought extremely sexy. There was no-one to appreciate this.

I lay on my stomach, breathing in the smell of my arms – salty flesh and sun-cream. If I looked up I could see rocks and steep fields. Thistledown floated and settled among the stones. A car arrived and I watched children climbing out with buckets and spades and a li-lo. I hoped they would find a spot far away, and yet at the same time I was lonely.

The sun was warm but I wanted it to be hot in that seductive, drowsy way that goes with lying on beaches sunbathing.

I sat up and looked out at the sea. It was ruffled by the wind. There were two clear colours, green and purple.

Where was I? In Ireland. It didn't seem like abroad but I felt strange here by myself on the beach. My father was happy with his melancholy pursuits. What was my mother doing? I had that childhood feeling of being left somewhere to play.

I put on my sweater and walked down to the water's edge. The sea rolled in, big green bottles, one behind the other. I thought of swimming but when I put my toe in it was cold. This was August. Why was it so cold?

I stood with the water breaking round my legs, feeling it pull the shingle under my feet. There was no-one near. If I went in and the currents took me I would drown, I told myself, turning my back on the waves.

I read my book and ate my ham sandwiches. Mary had been rather generous with the mustard. I thought about Julian and wondered if he would laugh at my solitary state, my reading matter, my wearing my bikini and then saying the water was too cold to swim in. I supposed I did miss him, but the truth was my mind was becoming increasingly empty and empty of him along with everything else.

Suddenly Tomas was there on the rocks in front of me. He was bending over a rock pool. He stayed there for some time; he was very still. Waves were breaking behind him and seagulls landing and taking off but he was motionless, a dark shape.

I returned to my book, wishing I had brought *Rebecca* instead. This one was too much about middle-aged people with snobbish ideas. I was beginning to notice this kind of thing in detective novels especially by women and it annoyed me, partly because I had been drawn into it at first. Bunnie and I used to play what we called the Lord Peter Wimsey game:

'*My dear Lord Peter, let me congratulate you on your wine-merchant.*'

'*And you on your tailor, my dear sir.*'

I was missing Bunnie and planning definitely to write to her that evening when two things happened at once.

First, there was a loud roar and suddenly a crowd of motorbikes were there, at the top of the beach. They were smoky and shiny; their riders wore black. There were just five bikes but they made a lot of noise, drowning out the sea and the shrieks of children. They turned off their engines and for a while there was silence. Then a child wailed. The bikers sat there and scanned the beach.

Second, Tomas appeared beside me. He sat, staring at the horizon, as if he'd been there all day. I searched for an opening phrase. I was more relieved than sorry that my bikini top was covered up. 'Nice to have the sun today' was making its way to my mouth when he said, 'What age are you?'

This was disconcerting as he still gazed straight ahead. Now I could see his profile at least.

'Sixteen. What about you?'

'Nearly eighteen. What part of England are you from?'

'The Midlands.' I was about to apologise for the Midlands as I so often did but then, in conversational terms the ball would hit the net and I felt he wanted me to keep up with his pace, so I said, 'I hear you're from Derry.'

He turned to face me at last. 'Who told you that?'

Is it a secret? I thought, but replied, 'Mary, I think. Your cousin.'

'Ah yes. Wee Mary.'

He seemed to have lost momentum. All through this exchange he had assumed control, his voice steady, even hard. But his right hand was scooping up sand and trickling it out again through his fingers.

The motorbikes started up, turned noisily and were away.

Tomas was silent. Then, 'What's your name?'

'Ellen.'

'Right, Ellen.' He got to his feet. 'See you later.'

What was wrong with him? He went to where the tide was coming in over the rock-pools. He moved gracefully and confidently, jumping from rock to rock. But he had left me feeling awkward. Was I so unattractive that he couldn't bear to sit beside me any longer? Or was it him? Was he so lacking in social know-how that he couldn't conduct an ordinary conversation? I had learnt nothing about him that I didn't know already. At least I had seen his face. He was quite good-looking only he frowned all the time.

6

It seemed ages before my father arrived to take me back to Miss Mulligan's. When we arrived he asked if he could come and sit with me. I thought this was a bit peculiar.

'It's everyone's sitting-room, isn't it?' I asked.

'Of course.'

He sat on the sofa and patted the seat beside him. I wasn't sure if I wanted him to cuddle me but anyway he didn't. He leaned forward and stretched his arms out in front of him with the fingers locked together.

'There's something you should know.'

He sounded very serious. *Oh no he's going to tell me they're getting a divorce.* I was careful not to show any panic.

'What? What?'

'Well it isn't really anything to do with us, but as we're living – well, staying at such close quarters...'

'Is it something about Miss Mulligan?'

'No. It's about Mrs Doherty and Tomas. Well,' he turned towards me, 'You've heard of the IRA?'

'Of course!'

'They mounted a campaign three years ago. It hasn't been very successful. Men lost their lives. One of them was Tomas' father.'

140

My shock felt like sudden fear. I didn't know what to say.

'Oh that's terrible! Poor Tomas!'

'Yes, and poor Ailish – Mrs Doherty. She's a widow. She's bringing up Tomas on her own, though her family are all helpful of course. He won a scholarship to a good school in Derry but it's still hard for her. She works in a shirt factory. For the holiday now, Miss Mulligan whose distantly related is very kind and she lets them stay here for nothing.'

'Ah poor Tomas,' I thought, 'Perhaps he doesn't really want to be here.' I tried to get a picture of their lives. 'Does Tomas have any brothers or sisters?'

'They've all grown up and gone away. Married. Gone to America. That sort of thing.'

'I see.'

'I thought you should know so that you'd know to tread carefully.'

'Yes of course. Well he does seem very serious all the time.'

'I don't mean you have to be solemn – just be yourself.'

There it was again; 'Be yourself.' According to the advice columns of women's magazines it guaranteed the success of all situations from first encounters to going steady. But what was 'myself'? I was grumpy and critical. Was this the way to

141

get along with strangers?

'I don't know what being myself is, but don't worry I'll be nice to him.'

He looked relieved and gave me a brief hug and told me not to be upset. Then I thought, 'Daddy? Is it still going on?'

'Well some people would say so. But we're safe here.'

Then he wanted to talk about the book he'd just borrowed from 'my' library, but I wasn't listening now because I was thinking how terrible it must be if one of your parents died.

At dinner I took a few glances at Tomas and his mother. I wasn't the only one. Mr Andrews kept looking at them. He had a way of watching people as they came and went and not only that but somehow letting it be seen that he was watching. It seemed out of the ordinary and as I now knew that Tomas and his mother were non-paying guests, I thought it extremely bad-mannered.

After dinner my parents said they were going out. In a nice enough way, they made it clear that it was just them, I would be staying behind. My mother suggested I might want to watch TV with the other guests.

I was in my room, not reading my book, wondering if I would brave the TV room when Mary came to fetch me. 'There's a cup of tea down below and we're watching "What's My Line". You coming?'

It was a small room with big armchairs. The television lit up the faces of Miss Mulligan, Mr and Mrs Andrews and Tomas's mother. My father was perched on the arm of the chair my mother was sitting in. In front of the TV a low table held an ashtray she shared with Mr Andrews. Mary served tea from a trolley at the side. I stood at the back. It was getting more and more like home when visitors came – sleeping on the sofa, nowhere to sit.

Tomas' mother stood up. She smiled at me and said, 'I was going anyway.' I said, 'Thank you' and slid into her seat, and my father added, 'Thank you very much.'

Mary stood entranced. Her face reflected all the puzzlement and laughter on the screen.

Miss Mulligan said, 'You may go home now, Mary.'

Mary became a child, saying, 'Can't I stay?... Me and Tomas...'

'It'll be getting dark. I don't want you walking home in the dark.'

My father leaned forward, 'Please forgive my intruding. I can drive Mary home. It would be an honour. Pat and I were planning a trip to the village anyway.'

My mother nodded and smiled at Mary. Miss Mulligan thanked them. Mary was delighted. When my parents left the room, Tomas came in and occupied their chair.

Now there was something Mary and Tomas looked forward to. It was a safari programme presented by a couple who were outlandish both in appearance and speech. We were introduced to blurred images of zoo animals in the wild. Mary and Tomas found it all very funny and before long I did too. Soon we were exchanging glances at every strangled vowel-sound and every anxious attempt to identify the foggy objects on the screen. I wondered at the abandoned laughter of Tomas who should be so sad. I was too young to understand grieving.

Mr Andrews kept clearing his throat. Eventually he and Mrs Andrews went away. And Miss Mulligan having gone some time earlier, the three of us were left, egging each other on to laugh at every opportunity and when these were exhausted Mary and Tomas repeated phrases until they were almost incoherent.

We lay back in our chairs pretending to be tired out with laughing. Suddenly Mary was talking about the motor cyclists. They had raced past here on their way to the beach. 'I was scared,' she said, 'Were you scared, Ellie, when they landed at the beach? Ah no, Tomas was there to protect you.'

Then my parents arrived and took her away. My father came and kissed me on the forehead. My mother was standing in the doorway, smiling. She gave me a little wave like a film-star or royalty. She looked smart in a coffee-coloured dress and cream duster coat.

After they'd gone, Tomas looked round the room and, seeing only me, he left quickly but he did say 'Good night, Ellen' on the way out.

What Mary said had started me thinking. At the beach, had Tomas come to protect me? It hadn't felt like that, but perhaps he was being tactful. Only what I began to suspect was that I had been protecting him. He had come to me with his clumsy interrogation, not to make friends but for shelter.

Was Tomas just a coward with no conversation? Perhaps he was still in a state of shock. I decided his nerves were bad and that I would not judge him too harshly.

7

Next day I wrote to Bunnie. I used the writing set she had given me for Christmas. Like the soap I gave her it was pink and scented. It didn't really suit the world I was living in.

The letter took a long time. It wasn't that I had so much to tell. The problem was the Three Lies. Compared with some of the people in our class, our holidays, mostly spent with our parents, seemed uneventful. Cousins with cars, midnight swims – we could not match these. So I decreed that in our letters to each other we were allowed Three Bold Lies. The recipient had to spot the lies and expose them in the return letter. Bunnie wasn't much good at it. She had no imagination so I got a lot of fun out of her pathetic efforts. 'I have gone completely blonde. I used my mother's hydrogen peroxide I found in the bathroom.' 'My father's friend from the war is visiting and he says I'm the most beautiful creature he has ever seen.'

My lies were more subtle, I thought. 'The good-looking man at the next table who keeps staring at me is Charles Aznavour.' 'I swam naked in the harbour last night.'

The trouble was when I tried to make up lies about Miss Mulligan's, they just wouldn't come. What could ever happen in 'my' room or at the beach to inspire fantasy? The sofa and chairs or the rocks at the shore had taken on a dull but pressing reality which left no room in my mind for play.

So I told her about Miss Mulligan and gave her a past, but even that was un-inspired. She had been a night-club hostess in London but had come home after an affair with a singer (lie number one).

I told her about Tomas but not about his father. I just said he was very good-looking (lie number two) and that he kept looking at me (lie number three).

Then I joked a bit about my father and his gravestones. I asked her to see what Julian was up to and ask him if he missed me.

'Must go.   I smell cabbage soup – again!
   Love from Ellie.'

Miss Mulligan very nicely found me a stamp and I posted the letter in the green letter-box.

Later I went for a walk.   I might have turned towards the sea, but there was a herd of cattle going down that road, moving very slowly.   So I took the road which led towards the mountain. I imagined climbing some of the way and looking down on the village and Miss Mulligan's and the fields in between and the road to the beach and the beach itself.

After a morning's rain the sun shone warm.   The road ahead was steaming and I could smell gorse in the hedge.   The leaves shone and all the flowers looked bright and wide-awake. There were whole bushes of brilliant red fuchsia.   Their flowers dangled like drop earrings.

I was glad to set out, to have a clear head after wrestling with words and confusing truth with falsehood in the gloom of Miss Mulligan's.   I was thinking about home and people I knew there and not at all about my new acquaintances.   Then after a bend in the road I saw Tomas' mother walking ahead of me.   I had been going quite fast but I slowed down, not wanting to catch up with her only she moved at such a snail's pace, I had difficulty keeping back.   Then she reached up to pick honeysuckle and, stepping back, she turned and saw me.

She waited, smiling with the same warm smile she had when she gave me her seat in the TV room. She was not in the least embarrassed, though I was. Then she moved on, glancing at me at her side as though to keep me there like someone walking along with a peaceable farm animal.

I wanted to speak but could think of nothing to say. I couldn't get it out of my mind that she had been violently widowed and that she was the mother of Tomas who was such a puzzle to me. I wouldn't say she chattered because that suggests something quick and bright. In fact she spoke slowly but about harmless things – how lovely it was to feel the sun, how beautiful the honeysuckle smelled. She was wearing a dress that had once been blue and pink but was now faded to a blurred mauve. She carried her white cardigan over her arm.

Another bend in the road and there was the chapel. She was going there and assumed I was too. Not wanting to deceive her I told her it was a long time since I'd been inside a church.

She seemed about to ask a question but then stopped herself, so I answered it anyway, 'We don't go to Mass any more.'

It was hard to explain why this was so without telling how my mother had started sighing whenever it was time to go and my sisters told her it was pointless going to Mass if she felt like that about it. So I just said something vague like 'things kept cropping up' and I omitted to mention that I had been told I could continue going if I wanted to, it was up to me.

'You poor wee thing,' said Mrs Doherty.

'Well Jennifer, my sister, she was married in church.'

'Of course, your father...'

'Oh I don't think he's anything really, maybe a bit of a Quaker.'

I was about to say, 'I think there's a lot to be said for the Quakers', but she was looking sad and rather sensitive and I told myself that her faith was probably a great comfort to her so I said no more. I thought I was protecting her feelings but it occurred to me much later that really I was intimidated by her certainty.

We went into the chapel together. I was happy to bless myself with the holy water. The smell of the interior reminded me with a shock of my childhood. Suddenly I seemed to have come a long way from there.

Only one candle was alight. She lit one and invited me to do the same, dropping money into the box. I was guessing that she lit hers for the soul of her husband. Mine was for my parents. Of course they weren't thinking of getting divorced, but I still wanted to bind them together in a blessing commanded by me (and paid for by Mrs Doherty).

She spent some time praying. I knelt at the back and breathed in the smell of wood and candles and thought my own thoughts which were a mixture of the devout and the heretical together with the usual day-dreams.

Afterwards we walked back to Miss Mulligan's. I abandoned the idea of climbing the hill. On the way I picked some flowers for my mother, little yellow ones like daisies and others which looked like thistles but without the prickles. Tomas' mother asked me about school and what subjects I liked. When I said 'French' she turned to me in excitement.

'So does Tomas. He loves French!' It seemed Tomas had a huge collection of French records and books and was trying to save to go to France. She asked if I had been in France and when I said I had she told me I must tell Tomas about it and talk to him in French. I said my mother spoke better French than me, but to that she only murmured politely.

I found my mother on a deck-chair in the garden shelling peas. She had her skirt hitched up to her knees to brown her legs. Before Mrs Doherty left us, the two of them exchanged pleasant remarks about the weather. I gave my mother the flowers. When I told her where I'd been, she said, 'I could have shown you the chapel.' Which surprised me.

There was no sign of Tomas.

8

It was dark and stuffy in my room. I tidied my writing case and paper then tried to open a window but they were all stuck shut. Still there was a slight draught coming through and I thought I could smell the sea. The wind was blowing straight at the house. The sea was visible now, a dark blue strip like metal.

I went downstairs and out of the front door. There was no one about. Our car and the Andrews' were still away. The layby was empty except for the flower bed with a few marigolds and weeds and grasses.

A car went up beside the house. Why would a car be driving into a field? But when I went to look I saw there was a lane I'd never known was there. It was narrow and had grass and daisies growing up the middle of it. On one side there was a wall made of stones and on the other a higher wall which was the side and back of Miss Mulligan's. It went up-hill and curved away under tall trees.

At first I thought I would just see where it went. It was late afternoon and very quiet. I could hear a tractor on the main road and insects close by. The trees kept out most of the sun but there was a broad patch of light up ahead. It felt like a secret place. The midges were bothering me so I tried walking fast.

When I reached the open part I found the sun was shining

on a golden field.   The gate was wide open.   It was a hay field with grass coming up through the stubble.   I walked through the open gateway looking straight into the afternoon sun.   It was like one of those peaceful landscapes in the paintings at Miss Mulligan's.   But there was a smell that reminded me of France.

Then I nearly jumped out of my skin.

'Hullo Ellen.'

Tomas was there!   He was sitting under the low hedge at the side of the field.   He was smoking a cigarette and looking very much at home.

'Oh you,' I said. 'You made me jump.'

'How do you think I felt?   Sitting here enjoying the peace...'

'I'm sorry.' Perhaps he was thinking about his father. Perhaps this was where he came to be alone.

'You're all right.   You can come and sit down if you want.   The ground's wet, mind.'

He was sitting on his grey sweater.   I found a large stone a bit away and perched on that.   It was warm but not very comfortable.   He took a packet of cigarettes from his pocket and offered me one.   *Disque bleu.*   I shook my head.

'I only just found this place,' I said.

'Oh I've been coming here for years.   It's nice.   Quiet but with plenty to see.'

To me it looked like everywhere else I'd seen in this country. Fields and hedges and a few trees.

'What is there to see?'

'Rabbits, look, and hares, and the sun going down.'

If Julian had said that I'd have assumed he was being funny. Rabbits and hares and the sunset! But when I looked at Tomas there was no sign of self-mockery. His face in the glow of the sun and without its usual angular tenseness seemed pleasant. There were all kinds of things I wanted to ask him. I was curious about his father and what had happened, but too nervous to ask.

'It's quite nice to get away from Miss Mulligan's,' I said but then remembered she was a relative.

He laughed. 'You can say that again!' but that was all.

I thought I'd better mention talking to his mother, because she was sure to and it would seem odd if I didn't.

'Oh yes. I suppose she was going to the chapel.' He said it neutrally but there was some feeling he wasn't letting through.

'Yes, we lit a candle.' I was looking at my feet and the grass coming up between my toes.

'Did she tell you all about me and how clever and hard-working and brilliant I am?'

I grinned and looked at him. I liked it when he laughed.

This was getting to be like a real conversation.

'Actually she told me you like French.'

'*Oui, c'est vrai, Mademoiselle. Et vous?*'

'Um. *Un peu.* I don't really speak it very well. My mother does. She's a French teacher. She's very fluent.'

'*Ooh la la!*'

'I was in France with the school two years ago. There were bombs in Paris.'

As soon as I'd said it, my heart sank. How could I be so tactless? But he just said,

'*Ah les bombes plastiques. "A toute a l'heure, plastiqueur!"* Did you ever hear that one?'

'Of course.' It was one of Julian's jokes, delivered in a Goon Show voice. I wondered if I should mention 'my boyfriend' but I was afraid that he might bring in 'my girlfriend' and that would close doors while now everything was so tentative.

He stubbed out his cigarette on the damp ground and rested his hands loosely on his knees. Then looking straight ahead of him in a way that reminded me of the beach, he said,

'*Je peux te tutoyer?*'

'Uh?'

'We can call each other "*tu*"?'

'Oh yes, of course.'

For me, '*vous*' was easier because I was used to the grammar. My mother never spoke French with me. I think she didn't want 'work' at home. I was thankful at least she and my father had stopped talking French when they wanted me not to know about something.

'*Elle est jolie, ta mere*,' said Tomas.

Jolie? My mother? Pretty? Well I wouldn't have used that word about her. She was nearly forty. Still I wasn't equipped to argue. '*Oui Tomas, tu as raison, je suppose.*'

He laughed. I didn't see why. I hoped we could return to English, so I asked, 'What other subjects do you like?'

'Nothing much. Well, I suppose history. And English some of the time.'

'I like English. What books are you doing?'

'Oh Dickens and Jane Austen, that kind of stuff. But I like French novels. Not the ones we do in school, things like *Madame Bovary* and *Cheri*.'

'I've never read a whole book in French in my life.'

'Really! But you could read Francoise Sagan, she's easy. You've heard of her all right, haven't you?'

'I've heard of her.'

'I'll lend you *Bonjour Tristesse*. You'll like that. It's easy read. And songs. Listen to songs. Jaques Brel, Juliette Greco...'

'Oh I do listen to Juliette Greco. *J'aime Juliette Greco.*'
I wondered if he would say I looked like her but now he started singing, very huskily, *Il n'y a plus d'apres...* and then stopped quickly, self-conscious about his voice. I would have found some way to reassure him but then I was shy as well.

Now the sun was in our eyes. It would soon be below the far hedge. I got up and pulled down my skirt. 'I'll be getting back.'

He didn't seem to mind. 'See you later,' he said, 'in the *salle a manger*, no doubt.'

Later in the dining room, Tomas' mother came in by herself. She smiled and we all smiled back. When Tomas came in, he looked neither to right nor left, and would not catch my eye. So much for '*tu*' I thought.

I had decided not to tell my mother about his compliment but then heard my voice saying, 'Tomas thinks you're *jolie*.'

'Does he indeed?'

'Young pup!' said my father.

'When were you talking to Tomas?' she asked.

So I told them about walking up the lane and meeting him in the field. I didn't say much about the conversation although they seemed curious to know how we got onto my mother being '*jolie*'.

'Oh he just said it.'

156

'In French?'

'He likes talking French.'

Then my father murmured something about a tradition in republicanism, links with the French and so on and I listened intently because his voice was low but I thought to myself that I couldn't really connect what he was saying with all that talk about Francoise Sagan and Juliette Greco.

It was stew today with lots of potatoes. We all ate heartily. My mother patted her stomach and said she must be putting on weight. My father said it was good for her and she said how nice it was, not having to do the cooking. I promised I would cook some meals when we got home. We were all in a good mood.

This was in contrast to Mr Andrews who left the dining-room early, his eyes fixed on the door, not acknowledging my father's smile. There was a large portion of stew remaining on his plate. Poor Mrs Andrews didn't even get a chance to drink her tea. My mother watched them from behind her smoke. She turned to my father, about to say something but then didn't.

The next day it rained. I got a notebook off my father and started up my diary again. Last term I'd decided to 'live life' instead of writing about it but now I wanted to record things again.

Is he good-looking? I wrote. *He is when he isn't frowning all the time but I admit to finding him intriguing when he doesn't smile. Does he have a sense of humour? A mild one, I suppose. But he doesn't make me laugh the way J. does. I wonder if J's cynical wit is his main appeal. I have been in physical contact with him many times at dancing but it wasn't really exciting though I did feel protected.* I paused to think about this. What did I feel protected from? Just the other boys who wanted to dance with me and were awkward I suppose.

There was a moment in the field when T. was singing rather self-consciously and then stopped and I wanted to touch him then and say something like 'It's OK you sound OK' but of course I didn't.

Will he remember to lend me that book? His enthusiasm is very appealing. I wonder if it's his way of not thinking too much about his father. J. has never had anything in his life as terrible as that.

My father came in and I closed the diary I hope not too obviously. He was in a great state of excitement.

'You'll never guess! What do you suppose Ailish Doherty's name was before she was married? Her maiden name.'

'I don't know. I can't think. Mulligan?'

'Dunne! She was a Dunne. Like my mother.'

'Well that's nice.' My Granny had died when I was too small to remember so the Dunnes were pretty remote to me.

'We could be related. And she came from Donegal. Of course half Derry came from Donegal. And,' here he lowered his voice, 'they were almost certainly Protestants.'

I felt as I had before, that my father had more access to my mother's world than she had herself.

Suddenly it occurred to me, 'Oh help! Tomas and I could be related.'

'Exactly. But why "Help!" Would that be so terrible?'

'Oh Daddy. No. But don't say anything to him. Please.'

His mother must have said something, though, because that afternoon, when I was searching the shelves for something to read, Tomas came in without knocking with a great grin on his face.

'Hello Coz.' He looked around the room. 'You've made it look different. Almost habitable. Is this where you sleep?'

I was embarrassed by my rolled-up bedclothes. I wished I could hide away my writing things and diary but I just said, 'Yes, I live here.'

'*Charmant.*' He was looking at the books then at the records all in a pile on the floor. 'I didn't know about these. Look what you've got! John McCormack – my mother's favourite. And Jean Sablon.' (Of course it was a man's name) 'and Schubert's unfinished symphony. And Smetana – you lucky girl!'

Sitting on the floor with our backs against the sofa, we filled the next few hours with music from Miss Mulligan's collection He was in a different mood again. Yesterday he had been knowledgeable in a matter-of-fact way about those French writers. Now he was loudly showing off, exuberant, even laughing. We played Jean Sablon singing *Stardust* and *Two Sleepy People* over and over again enjoying the French accent which Tomas then imposed on John McCormack for *The Kerry Dancing*.

'Don't let my mother hear us,' he said, 'it would be blasphemy.'

'Why?'

'She's a singer. All singers revere The Count.'

I giggled at 'The Count' but then, 'I didn't know she was a singer.'

'You should hear her. You will probably.'

'When? Soon?'

'Josie will be having one of her evenings soon. She'll sing then.'

'What sort of evenings?'

'You know, an evening. People come. She opens up

160

the bar and they come from all arts and parts and there's a bit of a session. Some fella with a melodeon and a fiddler, Jacky Doherty – no relation. Anyone can sing. Or do a recitation.'

'Sounds fun. Only I expect we'll miss it.'

'Why would you miss it?'

'We won't be here. We don't *live* here, you know.'

'So when are you leaving?' Was that a note of sadness in his voice?

'I don't know. They don't tell me anything.'

He was thoughtful. 'My mother tells me everything now. She would even consult me now. But they *never* told me what my father was doing. I knew nothing about that...escapade.' He was frowning again, the jagged, dark look had come back. I could think of nothing to say. Not being told when your holiday was over was nothing to not being told about your father's secret, dangerous activities.

He went back to the turn-table and now he was reflective rather than angry. 'I want to listen to this in memory of my father who loved it. It's Smetana. About his country. *Ma vlast*. This is the river.'

I sat looking at the floor. Tomas was very still. I could understand why the music had such meaning for him. It sounded hopeful and sad at the same time. There were parts which seemed to promise something wonderful. It was reaching for something. I didn't look at Tomas. By the end it was me trying to hide the tears coming into my eyes.

9

The next day it was not raining. There were big patches of blue sky. Tomas went off somewhere on his bike. My father took me to the beach and I made him promise not to leave me there too long. I was still wondering, as a sort of daily habit, how long we would be staying at Miss Mulligan's but now at last the sun was shining and the sea was deep blue and turquoise with just a few dashes of white. This time I went swimming and it was so cold I could hardly breathe. I kept looking and hoping Tomas would appear on his bike. I only wanted company. I was always lonely there.

Later both my parents came. My mother had brought a flask of tea. She was wearing a dark eau-de-nil sundress and already she was getting a tan which she did easily. Unlike me, one of the fair-skinned Aspinals like my father.

'You going in Mum?'

'Not today, dear.'

I was going to say, 'Why not, it's lovely' but then I thought perhaps it was that time of the month a thing I now knew about.

My father submitted his pale, angular body to the water and my mother laughed but in a friendly way when he came back shivering.

'Mum do you know about Miss Mulligan's evenings?'

'Of course. Everyone knows about Miss Mulligan's evenings.'

'So what happens?'

'Well, she opens up the bar and people come and drink and sing. Local people and any guests staying there who want to join in.'

'Will we be going?'

'If you like.'

'When is there going to be one?'

'Soon I expect.'

She turned away to brown her shoulders.

'Is it OK to go and not sing?'

She muttered something I couldn't hear. My father was not reassuring. 'You could do your party piece.'

'What party piece?'

'You know, the one about the little miller. "I care for nobody, no not I and nobody cares for me".'

I groaned and would have thumped him but if I had, he'd have tickled me and I didn't want that.

Later Tomas and I were playing *When They Begin the*

Beguine and he asked me to dance. When I said I couldn't he gave an exaggerated sigh of relief then closed the door and lit up a cigarette. He came to sit beside me on the sofa and we were shouting out the words together when the door opened and my parents came in.

Without a glance in our direction they began to dance. Their bodies swayed together in a way that I thought was lovely. Sometimes they looked at each other, sometimes away, never at us. Tomas tried to hide his cigarette at first but then let it burn between his fingers as he watched. My mother's skirt swayed against her legs. She leaned into my father's shoulder and let him lead the way. Tomas turned and looked through the records and it seemed almost rude, but when the dance was finished he joined me in clapping. I was quite embarrassed by how proud I felt.

My mother came and sat on the sofa beside Tomas, fanning herself with the cover of a record. 'Bold boy' was all she said about his cigarette.

He gave a quick laugh. 'That was very impressive Mr and Mrs...'

'Aspinal,' my father said.

I told them, 'I didn't know you could dance like that!' and my mother, acting mysterious, said, 'Ah there's a lot you don't know.' Then she got up and took my father by the hand and as they were leaving the room turned, 'You two should go for a walk in the fresh air. It's a lovely evening.'

But we stayed where we were. Tomas seemed to be smoking rather a lot. I started to hum *When They Begin the Beguine* but he didn't join in. Suddenly he said,

'Are you a virgin?'

I was speechless.

'Um. Well...'

'Oh come on Ellen, either you are or you aren't.'

'Well, yes I suppose.'

'Sorry, I didn't mean to embarrass you.'

'No, no I'm not embarrassed.' But why couldn't I ask him the same question?

He started to speak in a detached sort of way as though all this was nothing to do with him. 'It's a strange business, right enough. Of course the French have a far more civilised attitude to it.'

I waited.

'I mean their custom is for an older person to initiate the young person, someone experienced who would...'

I thought about what he was trying to say. 'Is it that I would be... deflowered... by an older man? Like one of my father's friends.' My mind ranged over this unappealing prospect. Thin or paunchy, pipe-smoking, bespectacled...

'Possibly.   And you see, I...'

'Oh no, someone like Mr Andrews, perhaps!   It's a terrible idea.'

'And I...well...who is the most attractive older woman here?'

'I don't know.   Miss Mulligan?'

'I said attractive, Ellen.   I mean lovely, womanly, firm and gentle.'

'I give in.'   This seemed like some fantasy creation.   'I don't see the point.   There are some girls in my school and their boyfriends, you know... they seem to manage being the same age.'   Things happened after school when I was stuck on the school bus, things I'd heard about and only half believed.

'Ellen. Concentrate.   The most lovely and sophisticated. French-speaking.'

'I can't think.'   I wished we could talk about something else.

'Come on Ellen.   Think.'

'Oh ye gods!   My mother?'

'You got there at last!'

'That's completely mad!   Don't be ridiculous.'

'What do you think?   She would, don't you think?'

'You're bonkers.   Of course she wouldn't.   She's married.   She's my mum!'

'I don't think your father would mind. He's a man of the world. Think about it. Just sound her out. I don't think she would be averse to the idea.'

'But you're so much younger. You're my age. She's my mother.'

I was laughing but he wasn't. 'Think about it,' he kept saying but every time he said it I laughed.

'I'm sorry there's no-one here for you,' he said and I agreed there was no-one for me. His eighteen months seniority would hardly count and besides I now suspected why he hadn't seemed at all interested in me physically.

I was relieved that he hadn't proposed me as his first. But I didn't like the way he didn't desire me at all. With my dark v-neck sweater and pale high cheekbones I thought he must surely find me interesting. Left-bank, maybe a little bohemian. I could accept that he was attracted to older women, but my mother? The whole thing aroused confused feelings in me. One of these was a new sense, deep as instinct, that I was physically undesirable, that I was considered immature, not ready for passion. Perhaps staying at Miss Mulligan's had made me lazy about my appearance. And my friendship with Tomas was not about wearing make-up or looking feminine. My jumper was flecked with grass seeds, my neck blotchy red where I had caught the sun and my hair felt lank and greasy.

The way he said 'Think about it' meant more than 'think'. He meant me to do something. There was a word for what he wanted me to do. What was it? I just knew it was out of the question. And my own mother! My aversion to the idea was deep and irrational but I tried to put into words what was wrong. It would be like serving her up in some way, was that it? I even felt protective towards her. And my father! There had to be limits to his niceness. I decided to put the idea out of my mind completely.

I knocked on my parents' door.

They were sitting up in bed side-by-side. My mother's hair was in rollers and she was wearing her cerise nightie with the plunging neck-line. She was reading and eating chocolates. My father in faded pyjamas, with his glasses on was busily writing something in a notebook.

'Where can I wash my hair?' I asked.

They hardly looked up.

'Your hair doesn't need washing,' my mother said, 'it's perfectly all right.'

'It's not. It's greasy and horrible.'

'It's grand, Ellen. It's not good to wash it too often.'

'But I haven't washed it since we left England.' I was beginning to whine.

'Daddy!'

'Robert, she says her hair is horrible.'

He looked at me. 'It's not at all horrible, my poppet. What a silly idea!'

'Well I want to.' I was childish. 'Where d'you get the chocolates?' I advanced.

'They were a present from Daddy.'

She looked at him fondly and he returned the look. She shifted onto an elbow and I could see the whiteness of her breasts where the tan ended. She seemed very pleased with things.

They were treating me like a child. If the door hadn't been slow to close like all the doors in Miss Mulligan's I'd have slammed it behind me. I went to the bathroom. I had no shampoo and now I couldn't ask for my mother's. I washed my hair with the pink soap and rinsed it with water cupped in my hands. It ran down my neck. I bumped my head on the taps. I knew they could hear me. I towelled my head and went to my room and to bed with wet hair.

They had no right to treat me like a child! She hadn't even offered me a chocolate. Later she appeared beside my bed and started telling me off about all the water on the bathroom floor. I pretended to be asleep.

A day later when things appeared to be normal again I went to her with a worried look on my face.

'Mum can you come...'

'What's wrong? Are you all right?'

'It's not me, it's Tomas. He's ill. He's got a fever and his mother's away to Derry all day. Can you help? He's got a terrible temperature.'

'How do you know? Where is he?'

'He's in their room. Please Mum, it's really worrying.'

'Is it something he ate?'

She sighed, but she did look concerned and then she went, without actually hurrying, to the Dohertys' room.

I stood on the landing. For a few minutes I continued to believe in the drama: a sick friend, a ministering angel. Quite quickly the enormity of it came to me. I tried to put out of my mind any picture of what might be happening but my mind insisted on dwelling on it. Would he explain in a reasonable way what it was he wanted or would he lunge at her, throwing off the disguise of sickness like the big bad wolf in grandmother's clothing?

Unhappy with my own company I went to the kitchen. Suppose my mother had gone there for water to put to his fevered lips. But all was as normal, Miss Mulligan sitting at the table making a list and Mary peeling spuds.

'Are you looking for your mother?'

'No. Yes. No, I mean she's not here.'

'She'll be here soon for a cup of tea. Will you not sit

170

down?'

But I fled.   I hadn't thought through what it would be like when I saw her again.   I began to feel raw guilt and shame. What had I done?   Procuring, that was the word.   Procuring my own mother for a person I didn't even care about.

I hurried out of the house and up the lane.   I walked on up past the field, trying not to think.   Of course she wouldn't necessarily know I had betrayed her – it could just be Tomas acting on his own.   But I knew.   No amount of thinking would change that.

The lane became narrow and muddy.   I turned back.   As I opened the front door, there she was, about to go up the stairs. She turned and looked at me.   All my life I had watched her closely without even realising it, to know if she was cross or pleased.   This time I couldn't tell.   She seemed to be smiling slightly as she said, 'I think we've taken care of your friend's little problem,' and then went on up the stairs.   At the top she turned again and said,

'You really should get more fresh air, Ellen.'

'Oh I just did.   I went for a walk.'

'Perhaps you should go out again.   It's going to rain soon.'

10

After this my mother was distant with me and gave the impression of being faintly amused whenever she spoke to me. I avoided Tomas and he avoided me. He never came to talk and play records. I didn't care. I couldn't imagine having an ordinary conversation with him. In the dining room he never looked our way. Mr Andrews had eased up a bit and even exchanged the odd joke with my parents. I thought of that conversation with Tomas and the idea of Mr Andrews being my 'older man'. The whole memory made me feel sick. The day after the Incident, I said to my father,

'I don't think Tomas can be related to us.'

'Oh really? Why not?'

'He just can't be.'

My mother raised her eyebrows and said nothing.

I tried not to keep wondering about what had happened but then a distraction came. Mary knocked on my door and looked round at the scattered records and the books pulled out and not put back and said, 'This place is wild looking Ellen. You'll need to get it red up before Miss Mulligan sees it. Here – a letter for you.'

It was in a brown envelope but behind the mad Gothic script I recognised Bunnie's writing. I started to tear it open;

Mary was still there.

'Is it a postal order?'

'No, no. It's just a letter. From a friend.'

I paused and at last she said, 'I'll go then and let you read it.'

'Thank you.' I gave a gracious smile. One of my mother's.

Dear Ellie the Heller. Sorry about the paper. I had to tear it out of my science book! No more science, hooray!!

It went on in this chatty pouring-out-everything style. She had been to see *Gigi* with her mother and sisters so now if Someone Else took her to it she would have to sit through it again. But then she probably wouldn't be seeing much of the screen!! She had decided not to go to 'Curlylocks' again because they always took off too much however you told them.

I had scant sympathy (as one of our teachers might say) for her troubles. She had bumped into some of the sixth formers from the boys' school who were bored with the holidays and they all went off to 'Causette' for frothy coffee and watched people walking by and made jokes and comments. At this I had pangs of something like homesickness or being-left-out sickness. No mention of Julian.

She had something to say about Tomas. *How is the tormented Tomas? I bet he never believes a word you say so*

173

that would make him Doubting Thomas! Ha ha Joke!

Nearly at the end of the letter, as if she'd just remembered him – Julian.

Julian has passed his driving test!! (This must be lie number one.)

He is going to take me for a spin in his father's car. (How could this possibly be true?)

Write again soon. How long will you be away?
Lots of love,
Bunnie

This was it? I looked for another page, maybe with a post-script. But there was no message from Julian, nothing about me at all. He couldn't have passed his driving test. Could he? All I'd heard from him were stories about beginning to learn and rolling downhill backwards, just avoiding a lady with a dog, nearly knocking over the headmaster's wife... But taking her for a spin? If he hadn't passed his test, and that must be a lie, then taking her for a spin had to also be a lie. That made two.

Now I re-read the letter for other possible lies. Did they go to *Gigi*? Had she really decided not to go to 'Curly-locks' where she really loved the fuss they made of her treating her like a grown-up, teasing her about her love life.

The whole thing was making me angry and confused.

174

She had obviously been talking to Julian. Or had she? And if so, why no mention of me? Then there were the references to Tomas. I would have to find a place to hide this letter. I had no privacy.

I drank tea in the kitchen. In front of my mother and Miss Mulligan, Mary asked,

'Was your letter nice?'

'Oh yes. Pretty nice.'

My mother turned. 'You had a letter?'

'Yes.'

'From Bunnie, I suppose.'

'Yes.'

Mary laughed. 'Bunnie?'

'My friend.'

'Not your boyfriend then? Sorry. Sorry, Ellen.'

'I haven't got a boyfriend.'

My mother was about to say something but refrained.

All this time Miss Mulligan was watching with great concentration. When I blushed she smiled at me and lifting the tea-pot said, 'Another drop of tea, Ellen?'

I nodded and as she poured she said, 'Mr and Mrs Andrews are for Tory Island today. I hope the rain holds off for them.'

She had changed the subject to help me. She must know

all about the sort of questions they were asking. About your private life, I thought, forgetting that hers had mainly been invented by me.

I re-read the letter but it only annoyed me more. Was Bunnie my friend at all? Next term I decided, I would spend more time with the serious people in our year and when it came to dancing-class I wouldn't always dance with Julian or laugh so much at his jokes. I had been drawn back so much into that world back home that I stopped wondering what had happened between Tomas and my mother.

Later that evening I went for a long walk under thick clouds but no rain. I had re-read the letter several times and it didn't get any better. I went as far as the chapel and walked on past it. In the hedges the flowers were looking dull and the hawthorns had their berries. There was a line of red beside the road where the fuchsia petals had fallen. I tried picking honeysuckle but they fell apart, all the petals tumbling down and catching on scraps of spider's web. I thought about next term and my new, serious friendships.

Back at Miss Mulligan's there was a room open near the front which was normally closed. Walking past I glanced in.

'Psst Ellen!'

Tomas was standing behind a small bar polishing a glass. 'C'mere.'

I stood in the doorway.

'Come on in.'

So this was the bar! There were chairs and stools and low tables on a violent red swirly carpet. Behind Tomas at the bar a collection of bottles – Lime juice, gin, Dubonnet, Martini, different kinds of whiskey. They looked old, not faded as in the sun but as if they'd been there a long time. There was a dusty smell and a smell of old beer.

'I've been sent to help. You want to help?'

He was his most smiling friendly self, inviting me as though it was his gift, to share some fun. I was disarmed by his generosity. And there was something conspiratorial about it.

Where would be the harm?

'Well OK. What shall I do?'

'Good. Good. Well now, how about the ashtrays. Here. I'll wash them, you put them round on the tables.'

He handed me a tea-towel and one after another the big clunky ash-trays. The tables needed dusting. He found a cloth. I noticed he was sipping at a glass of something light gold below the counter.

'A drink, *mademoiselle*? What'll you have?' He wiped the bottles and now they sparkled as I looked at them.

'I couldn't. How could I?'

'Come on. You're helping. A wee gin.'

'Oh all right then. Not gin. I'll have a Dubonnet.'

Apart from that one *'mademoiselle'* he kept away from French. Perhaps that civilisation had let him down. Now he had put the incident behind him and we were friends again.

He poured me the drink and said he was 'taking a break', bringing his drink to a table and lighting up a half-smoked cigarette. He patted one of the stools for me to sit near him. My drink seemed to go quickly; he refilled the glass.

The first drink had had no effect. With the second I began to feel a pleasant blur and the gradual lightening of my spirits so that Bunnie and her letter and the distant Julian no longer troubled me. I felt waves of sympathy for Tomas and his unrequited desires. I looked round the bar with its clean ashtrays and sparkling bottles. 'This is fun,' I said.

'Pity there's no juke-box.'

It may have been our singing or laughter that brought Miss Mulligan to the bar. She stood in the doorway and looked displeased.

'I was sent to help,' said Tomas, 'and then Ellie helped me.'

'You can finish now. Mary will do the rest,' and she left with a swirl of her skirt and her heels clacking towards the dining-room.

We suppressed our splutters till we were in 'my' room.

As well as his glass, Tomas carried his cigarettes and the whiskey bottle.

'Do you think you should? What if they find it's gone?'

'Ach there's plenty more. Go leor. Galore.'

He sprawled on the sofa. 'Give me music, Ellie.'

'Give me a drink, Tommy.'

The whiskey was harsh in my throat.

'D'you not like that?'

'It's strong.'

'Wait.'

He went away and came back with something sweet and fizzy to mix with it.

'There's just wee Mary down there. Being in charge. Very much in charge. Checking the stock, so she is. Here. A cocktail! We have no ice. There is no ice. Only in the heart of one who shall be nameless.'

He must like me, I thought, *to go and get that*. So I pretended to like the cocktail.

I don't remember much about the rest of the evening, but I have a vivid picture of him trying to dance to the South American Medley. He would fling himself about the room, coming back to me, grabbing my hand and straightaway letting it go again. I tried to dance as well, in the only style I knew, the Friday afternoon dancing class.

'You are a square, Ellie, the way you dance, d'you know that?'

'I don't care. As long as there's music and moonlight and love and romance...'

I remember trying to quench my thirst with the whiskey 'cocktail' and only feeling more thirsty. He filled my glass.

'Let's just listen,' I said, 'to the divine Jean Sablon,' but Tomas had disappeared. I waited for him and then slept a while. When I woke I was still alone. I put on *When They Begin the Beguine* and danced by myself, crossing the room in great swoops. I sang nonsense words with 'Bravo' and 'Ole' and clicked my fingers. It made me thirsty but when I took a gulp of The Drink it tasted so disgusting I rushed to the bathroom and poured it away. I tried to be sick but couldn't. The drink would be with me for some time.

I wanted someone to talk to. My parents were sitting tucked up in bed under the swirly patterned eiderdown. I felt they had put up a barrier against me.

'Hello you two!'

They were both reading. My mother had one of those green detective novels.

'How's everyone in here?' I asked loudly sprawling backwards on top of their clothes on a chair.

'Ellie!' my mother said rather snappily, 'Come here!'

'No you come here.'

'Ellen! What have you been doing? Have you been drinking?'

My father looked up. She continued her questions.

'Have you been out somewhere? Where did you drink? Was Tomas with you?'

'Oh Tomas, Tomas! Have you noticed he has a wild way of disappearing! He will disappear out of our lives you know.'

'Ellen you're babbling. Where did you get drink?'

'In the bar, where else? The establishment has a bar. It's very nice. I had a cocktail.'

Now my father showed real interest.

'The bar. Is the bar open?'

'Don't be ridiculous Robert.'

'It is open. Shall I get you a drink, Daddy? What would you like? If I can just find the barman.'

'Oh no no. And no more for you either.'

'Go to bed, Ellie, and drink plenty of water first. Come here.'

This time I went to her and she kissed me and repeated about the water.

Then I went to the Dohertys' room downstairs, back behind the kitchen, looking for Tomas. I knocked on the door and that gentle voice said 'Come in'. I was surprised to see she was lying on a folding bed and the big bed was empty.

'Why are you on that bed?'

'To sleep. Why not?'

'And Tomas sleeps in that big bed all by himself?'

'It's best this way. Tomas is that much taller than me. He can stretch out.'

'Well Mrs Doherty, Ailish, I think you are a saint. A real saint. No no I'm not expecting you to agree. I just want you to know I think you are a perfect absolute saint.'

She lay there resting on her elbow, looking quite awkward as I loomed in the doorway. I looked at the empty bed where Tomas' pyjamas, black stripes like a prisoner, lay waiting for him.

'Where's Tomas?' I asked

'I thought he was with you.'

'Insofar as he ever will be, he was. But then he went.'

I didn't want her to worry. 'He didn't drink much.'

'Oh no he doesn't drink. But... Are you all right Ellen?'

'Yes, I'm perfectly fine. I'll say goodnight now.'

'Goodnight, Ellen.'

Upstairs I rinsed out the drinks tumbler and filled it again and again from the bathroom tap and drank. I'd never felt like this before. My face in the tiny, mottled glass looked familiar and yet quite strange.

On the landing I bumped into Mr and Mrs Andrews.

'Good evening, Mr and Mrs Andrews. Did you have a pleasant evening?' I knew my voice sounded loud.

'Very nice, thank you,' said Mrs Andrews.

'You should go to your bed, wee girl,' said her husband, moving quickly towards their room.

I didn't like his tone. I felt like going to complain to my mother, 'He talks to me like his social inferior', but their door was closed and I was beginning to feel tired.

I put on *Two Sleepy People* and got into bed and was asleep before the end.

11

I woke before dawn. Awake instantly with a dry mouth and my head sore each time I moved, I began to worry. Bunnie and Julian. Tomas – why did he keep not being there? Did his mother really not know he drank?

I got up and walked around and drank more water from the bathroom. The sound was amplified. The house was very quiet. I tried to read but couldn't even get to the end of a sentence.

This must be a hangover. So why did people boast about it?

I looked out at the misty grey fields and saw Mary arrive. She had walked from the village without looking puffed. She wore blue slacks and a windcheater. How could she look so much more grown up than when we first arrived?

I crept down to the kitchen. She had a kettle heating on the gas and was cleaning the ash from the range.

'Mary.'

'Ellie! What are you doing up?' She looked at my bare feet.

'Any chance of a cup of tea?'

'Are you not foundered in your bare arms?'

'Freezing.'

'Go back to bed. I'll bring your tea.'

Climbing the stairs I thought she seemed disapproving. What had happened to the wonder and admiration of our first encounters? Then I pictured the state of my room and I rushed to get on a sweater and sandals and returned to the kitchen, saying, 'Can I stay here with you, Mary?'

'All right, only I've a lot to do.'

I sat there in a daze and watched as she set the fire in the range and put a match to it. Sparks came up when she opened the top and piled in turf. She took out the ash and a cat came in and she shooed it out. The swallows set up a twittering.

I said 'Aah' in a sentimental voice.

'Aah nothing. It's a wee divil.'

My senses were very clear and yet I was distant from them. I watched her make the bread, weighing the different flours in a jug, measuring buttermilk, working quickly, making a cross in the loaves before they went into the gas cooker.

The kitchen was beginning to warm up. I felt sleepy.

'I'm off back to bed now, Mary. Thanks for the tea.'

'It's well for those who can go to their beds at this hour,' she said, and let the cat in.

That's what I knew you'd say, I thought. I heard Miss Mulligan's door open so I crept quickly up the stairs. I shivered under the blankets and eiderdown and my feet were cold. The whiskey bottle. I worried that Tomas would be in trouble. It stood guard over the black choppy lake of gramaphone records.

Then I knew what to do with it and filling it in the bathroom, I wrapped it in a sweater and it had become my jar. The word my mother used and made my friends laugh. I lay with my feet against it, curled up like a baby inside its mother, pressing a hand down on top of my head to soothe the pain. My mind skidded over my worries. Bunnie and Julian as I lay on the side facing the windows, Tomas when I turned to the wall. I felt a certain tenderness for him, that's how I described it. I hoped he wasn't in the IRA. Did his mother really not know he drank? All these thoughts just swam in and out of my mind like

185

little fishes. I didn't even try to net them.

I might have dozed over only my mother came.

'How are you feeling?'

'OK. Thanks.'

'Are you coming to breakfast? What's that bottle doing?'

'It's me jar. Me feet were foundered.'

That brought a smile. 'Well come on down when you're ready.'

Mary wasn't pleased when I refused bacon and eggs. Even the new bread was hard to chew.

I went that day with my father to a distant graveyard. Staying at the entrance I watched in a dream while he made his way through long grasses to peer at old names. Old crumbling names. As he crouched there his lonely figure moved between past and future in my mind. I would remember this image when it was part of my history, always, for the rest of my life. I was a blank that day; but things were impressed on my mind.

How could he spend his holiday in these places with their brambles and grey stones without always being sad?

My headache was lifting. He asked me how I was feeling and I said 'a bit spiritual'. We stopped at a bar in a small village. He ordered a glass of Guinness 'and a port for the lady.' Watching the barman pouring and patiently scraping the top of the stout then pouring again while I sipped my port, I felt calm and almost content. There was a turf fire just lit in the grate, smoking. I had begun to love that smell.

'When will we be going home?'

'Very soon, my love, very soon.'

It was a small bar, smaller than Miss Mulligan's, and very quiet. Two old men in caps sat together in a dim corner without talking. The man behind the bar smoked and read a paper.

I was sitting with my back to the door and didn't notice the new man come in. I only saw his back as he leaned on the bar. He turned round and suddenly I felt exposed. His hair was inky dark. He was just wearing a white shirt over jeans and you could see his chest and face and how brown he was. He leaned back against the bar, his drink in his hand, completely easy. It was as though his limbs flowed.

I wasn't in the habit of thinking of men as beautiful. Women were; men were supposed to be strong-jawed and handsome all right but we were the beautiful ones to be admired. A beautiful man would be something a sculptor would make. This man, I wanted to keep looking at him, but the raw, nervous way I was feeling, I just stared at my drink and heard my heart thumping in my ears.

One of the old men called over to him.

'You home then, Micky? Where were you this time?'

187

'Scotland. Digging drains.'

'Be Christ, were you? Tell me this...' then something I couldn't understand.

This Micky took his drink over to join them. He definitely looked at me as he walked past and I smiled but he was already on his way. I blushed.

My father finished his glass. 'Ready?'

Now I wanted to stay. As we were leaving, the old man who had called out before, asked, 'Would you be staying at Josie Mulligan's?'

'Yes, yes, we are.'

'Is there a bit of a session the night?'

'Yes, I believe there is.'

The old man turned to Micky.

'Will you go?'

'I might. Yourself?'

'If she wants me to play. She'll have to ask?'

Everyone in the bar laughed. We smiled politely and my father said, 'See you later, perhaps.'

12

She must have asked the old man because in the evening he was sitting there with a black squeeze-box on his knee. Not wearing his cap he didn't look so old now at all. He had a different companion, a fiddler. They were playing a few quiet notes; the fiddler was tuning up. There was no sign of the dark-haired man who had been in Scotland – and in my thoughts for most of the afternoon.

I wandered between the bar and the kitchen. Miss Mulligan and Mary had been making sandwiches; they were all set out on the kitchen table. In the bar, Mary was serving bottles of beer and stout while Miss Mulligan chatted graciously to everyone who arrived. She looked very striking in a swirling red skirt. I was in the way, there was nothing for me to do.

Up in my room I found Tomas smoking and frowning.

'Are there many arrived?'

'Two musicians, one with a...' (I mimed an accordion)

'... melodeon, most likely.'

'And a man with a fiddle. And a few other people I don't know. The musician's friend isn't here.'

'Who's that?'

'Micky someone. He's been in Scotland digging drains.'

'That could be anyone round here, Ellen. How do you know him? What's he look like?'

'I don't actually know him (yet). He's tallish, dark, very tanned'

'Well he would be, would he not, digging drains?'

I didn't like the way he said that, it sounded almost

contemptuous, but I couldn't form a reply before he was asking, 'Are the Andrews couple there?'

'No, nor my mum and dad. Nor your mum.'

'My mother will be there – she's going to sing.' He drew hard on his cigarette.

'Are you feeling nervous for her?'

'She's a total innocent, my mother.'

If we went to the window we could hear the hubbub from below. Then the music started, Irish music, that lilting, foot-tapping music which I loved.

'Oh come on Tomas, let's go down.'

'You go, bring me up a drink.'

The bar was getting crowded. My parents and the Andrews were there. Through the smoke I could see the musicians, and behind them, turned so he was in profile – him! He wore the same shirt, his hair lay wet on the collar. I was pleased that he had got ready to come. He was leaning close over the drum as though listening to it. The other two were smiling at each other and at the rest of the room as they played but he was all serious concentration.

He has stolen my heart away. That's how I said it to myself.

While Mary was giving me a bottle of beer for Tomas and lemonade for me, there was a pause in the music and she said,

'That's my other cousin Micky, playing the bodhran.'

'Is he your cousin too? Oh he's . . .'

'Aye and all the girls are dying about him.' Some of her old boastfulness was back.

I took Tomas the beer. 'I think he's your cousin. Well he's Mary's cousin. He's here playing some kind of drum,'

'Bodhran (it sounded like boron). That'll be Micky an Touras.'

'Not a Doherty then?'

'Yes, that's their nickname.'

I always thought nicknames were like 'titch' or 'carrot-top' or like Bunnie because of her front teeth but he started to explain how in the big clans the families had to have special names because there were so many of them but then he lost interest and said, 'I'll explain another time' and I was eager to go downstairs again. I would stand at the bar, being friendly to his cousin Mary and force Micky by my will to look at me.

'Want anything downstairs?' I asked Tomas.

'No, don't go, Ellie.'

He put out a hand without reaching me. I was still touched.

'Are you afraid of crowds?' I asked.

'Yes. Yes. I am. Too many people . . .'

The music stopped. The bar went quiet. Someone

seemed to be reciting a poem. Then a hard, clear voice started to sing.

'Sh h... it's her − it's me ma.' He opened the door to listen.

'It can't be her,' I thought, '*her* voice is sweet.' I could just hear the words; in the background, the drum was sounding very soft.

> But the leader was a Limerick man
> Sean South from Garryowen

Suddenly – uproar. A man's voice was shouting. The singing stopped. More shouting and Tomas was downstairs like a shot. 'It's that Orange bastard! I'll kill him!'

There were cries of outrage. I followed on down and there was Mr Andrews with a red face, rising from his seat. His shoulder was restrained by his wife and at his feet Miss Mulligan had sunk to the floor like a ballet dancer, her circular skirt making a red pool, with her in the centre. Her white frilled blouse showed her breast rising and falling in agitation. 'No sir, you must stay.'

'I didn't come here to listen to this – treachery! No party songs! There should be no party songs here!'

She spoke softly, at which he shouted even louder, 'Is it my fault she's a widow? Who widowed her? Did I widow her?'

There were murmurings in the bar. I tried to make out who they were sympathetic to. He repeated 'No party songs' in an almost self-righteous way.

Then my father approached him. 'On the contrary, sir, why not sing something from your own tradition. I'm sure we'd be happy to hear one.'

'What tradition? What tradition are you talking about?'

'Give us The Ould Orange Flute!' someone shouted.

Micky was now helping my mother and Tomas to comfort Ailish; she was in tears. For a moment they looked like a group in a religious painting. I wanted to join them but then Mary came from behind the bar and stood in front of Mr Andrews who was now seated. Without pleading, she said, 'Come on Mr Andrews |I know you can sing.'

'I don't know any of them Orange songs. I am not sectarian.' At this another murmur from the company and a sort of yelp from Tomas. Mary went on.

'You know you look very like Frankie Vaughan. Could you not sing *When you walk in the garden*? Jackie!' she called to the melodeon player, 'You know it.'

No-one seemed surprised to hear the first bars of *When you walk in the garden* and then Mr Andrews stood up and closed his eyes. The music was soft, patient, giving him time. The group nearest the door shifted position and made room for two men in black motorcycle gear carrying helmets. They went to stand near the bar then, like everyone else, looked towards Mr Andrews.

13

He knew all the words and had a strong voice. He sang in tune and with dramatic passion. As soon as he opened his eyes he looked down at Miss Mulligan who had now moved to a stool. He gazed at her

> *When you walk in the garden,*
> *In the Garden of Eden*

and all the stuff about a beautiful woman, his eyes most intense with

> *And a voice in the garden*
> *In the Garden of Eden*
> *Says she is forbidden*
> *So you leave her there.*

I felt myself blushing for her but when I took my eyes away from the floor she was sitting looking at him with that delighted fixed smile of hers. Some male voices in the room made encouraging noises.

There was generous applause. Only the fiddler was scowling and a couple of others looked as if they would prefer not to be there. The motorcyclists muttered to each other. My heart sank when I turned and saw that Tomas and his mother and his cousin Micky had gone.

Miss Mulligan rose and thanked the singer and smiled hard at his wife, then went to the bar where Mary was grinning in triumph and serving the men in black. Miss Mulligan left and as soon as she was in the passage outside I heard Tomas' angry voice, 'Why should he be allowed to sing and not my mother?' and quieter words coming from his mother and Miss Mulligan and a man's voice which must have been Micky's but I couldn't make out the words. When would he come back? And then Tomas again, 'These people have it all! Everything!'

I sat with my parents. When the music started up again it was all jolly and hearty and about wild rovers and fine girls. Feet were stamped but Miss Mulligan's carpet gave out little in return. There were no more solos from Mr Andrews but he joined in loudly with *You are my sunshine* when he gazed at his wife as passionately as he had earlier at Miss Mulligan. And *The Tennessee Waltz* – he knew that. There was one I liked, *The Black Velvet Band* , but most of the time I wished they would sing a sad song, something mournful and lovely. I was sure Ailish would know one but of course she didn't come back and neither did Tomas or Micky. A young fair-haired boy was playing Micky's drum only without the same dedication. The motorcyclists tapped out the rhythms on their helmets.

My parents looked glum and didn't join in. I was glad when it was time to go to bed. Climbing the stairs behind them I heard my mother saying something about her, I supposed Miss Mulligan, being a business woman and my father murmuring what sounded like excuses.

The next morning at breakfast, Mr Andrews crossed the room with his hand held out to Mrs Doherty and she took it with a grave look. I thought it as well Tomas wasn't there.

I heard him, though, shouting in Miss Mulligan's room,

'Is it because he's paying and we're not that we have to go? He's the one should go. He was ignorant about my mother's singing. That's nothing to you though is it?' I climbed on up the stairs and he was talking about Mr Andrews disrupting the party. Then Mary chipped in, 'No. Everyone was singing. He had a fine voice.'

'Singing? Songs like that? Why does everyone let a man like that take over?'

'Would you rather French songs that nobody understands?'

I felt sorry for him. He seemed to have no friends in Miss Mulligan's. I hesitated on the stair but I hadn't the courage to go and help him.

A little later my parents told me that we would be leaving later that day.

14

This is not real pain, I told myself. I knew there would be worse because of what they said in books and songs. But it was still pain. I had fallen in love at first sight and now I was being taken away before we had even spoken or our hands touched. And my friend –Tomas. I was still confused about Tomas. I had expected him to come and say goodbye and help me put away the records and we might listen one more time to Smetana's lovely music about his country. And we could talk. *Peace is best isn't it*, I had planned to say, *it's better that your mother and Mr Andrews shook hands*. I was passionate about peace. We were reading Wilfred Owen at school ... *'the old lie, Dulce et decorum est pro patria mori'* and Julian wore a CND badge and was allowed to go on the Aldermaston march but my parents had said I was too young.

Tomas did not come. My mother found me in tears looking at the books and records all in disorder on the floor. She put her arm round me and said gently, 'Would you like me to help you with that?' the way she used to when I was a child.

.

AN HOUR IN THE LIFE

Martin Philpot lay on the floor of his office slowly returning to consciousness. He had taken the large square cushions from the university-issue Scandinavian chair and these made a mattress for the upper part of his body. The lower part needed no padding. He looked at his watch. Quarter to four. Christ almighty! They would be arriving in fifteen minutes!

He pulled himself to his feet with the grunt which had become the normal accompaniment to any physical exertion. Every so often he would notice it and resolve to grunt inwardly, or even, when he was feeling particularly ambitious, not to grunt at all. It was such a give-away. He returned the cushions to the chair and drew the curtains, flinching from the sunlight as it dazzled on white tiles. The taste in his mouth indicated coffee but he had still not prepared his class. It was his first meeting with a new batch of students. A good impression might carry him several weeks into the term.

He made a desultory attempt to tidy his table, and groaned to realise how little he had read of the Ph.D. thesis he was currently examining, *Spokespeople, The Bicycle in Anglo-Irish Literature* by Sister Basil Murphy. How could she have written so much? And so far there were very few redeeming shafts of humour. Even *The Anglo-Americanness of Malcolm Lowry* had been less dreary. Life on the fringes of English Literature was not always the fun he pretended it was to his colleagues. And he heard terrible rumours of some dreadful people living less than a hundred miles to the West in a converted lighthouse who all wore smocks and called themselves the Hiberno-Cornish group of writers. He belched gently, re-savouring the brandy which, with the help of Sister Basil, had sent him to his brief oblivion. A private familiar feeling of self-disgust washed over him. It had been sheer greed which had made him accept the Dean of Communication Studies' offer of 'something a little stronger'. Greed. Gluttony. 'You think it terrible that lust and greed... Are compensation for this loss of seed.' No. Ambiguous but totally misleading. That was hardly the problem. 'You think it terrible that something – air/Are compensation for this loss of hair.' 'You think it terrible that tum-ti-tum...'

Martin stood in a trance for some seconds and then made his way via the lift to the 'coffee bar' on the ground floor. Here a machine promised to dispense black coffee, black coffee with sugar, tea, tea with sugar, hot chocolate, soup. He selected black coffee with sugar then felt vainly in his pockets for the necessary 5p piece. He searched both pockets. Enough 10ps and 2ps for a phone call to the remote Bermudas but no 5. Now what? He turned and faced the seating area and recoiled in his customary fastidious horror. Hundreds of plastic cups, chocolate wrappings, pools of spilt coffee decorated the shiny tables. No sign of any of his colleagues, just corduroy or denim-clad figures scattered here and there. He approached the nearest, a lad with dark, curly hair sitting alone reading. He looked slightly familiar.

'Hm. Excuse me, have you a five-p piece?'

The boy leaned back and reached with difficulty into tight pockets. The coins he took out included a 5p.

'Ah, thank you. Now I have several two-ps but no one-p, but I can let you have…'

'No you're all right.'

'No no, here you take 6p. You're doing me a favour… Oh, I say, this appears to be an Irish coin. Still, I doubt if the machine will object. Thank you. Most kind.'

'You're OK. Can you tell me the time?'

'Nearly five to four.'

'Dead on. Thanks.'

The machine did indeed accept the coin but rewarded him with a murky grey substance. It was hot and he shifted it from hand to hand as he returned to the fifth floor. As the lift came to a halt a large proportion of liquid spilled out, scalding his hand. There were now five minutes in which to prepare his class. Back in his room he found a pink memo from the registrar about dogs on the campus, placed the weeping plastic cup on it, then wiped his fingers on another memo from his head of department announcing that all deadlines for essays were to be strictly adhered to.

Now which poem? As he was unprepared it would have to be something he knew quite well but which would cause them some difficulty thus allowing him time to collect his thoughts. He fumbled through his file of cyclostyled sheets. Ah! Empson. 'Missing Dates'. *Slowly the poison the whole bloodstream fills.* He read it through rapidly. Now what was that about the Chinese tombs? Empson had an explanatory note which he could read to them after he'd kept them guessing for a while. He searched the shelves for his copy of Empson. No sign of it. Why did nobody ever bring back books? He returned to the poem and reading it through again was filled with panic. What on earth did the bloody thing mean? There was a time, when his marriage was breaking up, when he had been convinced it was about failed relationships. Now it seemed to be nothing of the sort.

There was a knock at the door.

'Yes?'

It was the Irish student. Had he come, Martin wondered absurdly, to return one p? But he looked equally surprised.

'Are you Dr. Philpot then?'

'I am indeed.'

'I think we've a class with you now.'

'Yes, well, look could you wait outside for the others? Oh they're here. All right come in.'

They filed in, taking places with the awkward courtesy of people sitting down together for the first time. Martin continued to search his file, but now he was trying to give the impression he knew what he was looking for. Gray's Elegy? They'd probably done that at school. *To His Coy Mistress*? Somehow he didn't feel he could do it justice today. Perhaps a General Discussion of the What are We Here For variety. What is a work of art? What is the critic's role? Is he a parasite or a much-needed... Ah! Saved by the Bard, no less.

'I thought,' he said casually, trying to put himself at ease, 'we'd kick off by taking a look at one of Shakespeare's sonnets. "They that have power to hurt and will do none".'

He handed out the sheets.

'First, though, I'd better get to know who you are. Let's

see, I have a list somewhere.' He searched the papers on his desk. 'Ah, here we are. Mr. Hamilton, Miss Kirkham, Miss Martin, Mr. O'Reilly, Mr. Sillington-Kirby. Is that right?'

There was a murmur of assent.

'But there appears to be somebody missing. Not a very good start. Perhaps he or she has transferred to something more exciting, more relevant even, like sociology.' He smiled but no-one seemed to understand his joke.

'Right, Mr. Hamilton?'

'That's me.'

'Oh yes, I remember now. From Londonderry.'

The provider of the shilling was the student who, at his interview, had declined to talk about Flann O'Brien and chosen Dostoevsky. A serious youth.

'Well I expect you'll find it quieter here. Now, Miss Kirkham? Are you Miss Kirkham?'

'No I'm Susan Martin.'

'Oh yes. All right. No Miss Kirkham. Perhaps she's overslept.' This time there was a little giggle from Susan Martin. 'Well, people do, you know,' he went on, 'even at this time of day. Now then. Miss Martin. Yes, we've got you. Mr. O'Reilly. Hm. Another Irishman. What is this? A plot?'

'Actually, I'm from Liverpool.'

'Well you know what they say about Liverpool.' Martin

shifted his large bulk in his seat but managed to suppress a grunt. 'Never mind. Er... Mr Sillington-Kirby.'

'That's me. People call me Sime.'

'Sime?'

'Yes, you know, short for Simon.'

'Well Sillington-Kirby is a mouthful but I shall go on calling you that until we know each other better. As of course we will, all know each other very well by the end of this academic year. Now we meet each week at this time. I expect you to attend every week. You won't, of course, but I shall be expecting you. We shall learn how to read a poem, or a piece of prose, and what criticism is about, what we are all here for. We'll start with this sonnet. I'm going to give you five minutes to read it through and then we shall discuss it.'

They turned to their pieces of paper and Martin sipped his coffee. Vile stuff and now scarcely warm. He looked at them in turn. Nearest the wall was Hamilton, frowning slightly. He had not smiled at Martin's pleasantry about finding England quieter, and to Martin this made him slightly threatening. 'Obviously a boring fanatic like the rest of them,' he thought. The Liverpool one next to him looked nice. Very young, with a look of malleable receptivity which was reassuring. The girl, Susan Martin, was extremely pretty. A suburban version of Janey Morris with dark wavy hair, she wore a dress covered with tiny flowers. Her cast-down eyes showed long lashes. Demure. A virgin still? He had chosen her for his group by referring to the runic scribblings on the card index system he used when interviewing sixth-form applicants. A useful system of initials known only to himself usually secured him the pretty ones. Harrison could have the chess players and Baring the singers of madrigals but he had other hobbies, he would tell them. Pity the other hadn't turned up. Perhaps she had transferred to Environmental Studies.

Sillington-Kirby or 'Sime' was looking ostentatiously round the room casting his eyes over the Beardsley print and the rows of books. He assumed a pose of exaggerated puzzlement on arriving at the diagram on Martin's blackboard. This appeared to show a number of interlocking triangles enclosing two broken springs. Underneath were the words 'perne in a gyre'.

'I take it, Mr Sillington-Kirby, that you understand the poem fully.'

'We did it at school.'

'Well take another look at it. I shall expect a brilliant exposition from you.'

The youth sighed and turned back to the poem. He had discarded a very grubby once-white Afghanistan coat to reveal an equally grubby suede shirt with fronds of leather hanging ·

from each pocket.   More leather objects dangled round his neck. His hair which was mouse-coloured hung long and lank.   He had the beginnings of a moustache.   Father's occupation: judge, his form had said, which was why Martin had chosen him for his group.   Not because he was a snob in the old-fashioned sense but for the same reason he had chosen Michael Hamilton whose father was a plasterer, because he always liked a bit of class tension in his seminars.   Nothing duller than the children of bank managers all agreeing with each other he would tell Baring and Harrison.   His colleagues, inevitably left with such 'rejects' after Martin, chief selector, had picked through the pile, would assure him that their students rarely agreed, that their classes were lively and provocative, but Martin chose not to believe them.   He turned to the poem and read it through once.

> *They that have power to hurt and will do none,*
> *That do not do the thing they most do show,*
> *Who, moving others, are themselves as stone,*
> *Unmoved, cold and to temptation slow;*
> *They rightly do inherit heaven's graces*
> *And husband nature's riches from expense;*
> *They are the lords and owners of their faces,*
> *Others but stewards of their excellence.*
> *The summer's flower is to the summer sweet,*
> *Though to itself it only live and die,*
> *But if that flower with base infection meet,*
> *The basest weed outbraves his dignity:*
> *For sweetest things turn sourest by their deeds;*
> *Lilies that fester smell far worse than weeds.*

'Is it OK if we write on these, or do you want them back?' asked O'Reilly.

'Feel free. They're all yours. Do what you like, though I should be saddened to see them made into paper darts and thrown round the refectory as seems to be the custom in this institution.'

All except Sillington-Kirby began to jot conscientiously. Martin found Empson, not Shakespeare, sounding in his head. *The waste remains, the waste remains and kills.* He returned to the sonnet.

'Mister Sillington-Kirby, I should be grateful if you wouldn't tip your chair back like that. It isn't that I would necessarily mind if you fell over backwards but I find it most distracting. I think it's time we looked at the poem.'

'Now who will tell us what it's about? Mr. O'Reilly?' He had no intention of asking Sillington-Kirby, not only because he wouldn't give him the satisfaction, but because if Sillington-Kirby did indeed expound the poem correctly there would be none of the tentative gropings and discussion on which he was depending. But O'Reilly spoke with confidence.

'Well it's a difficult poem because Shakespeare doesn't seem clear at first whether he likes these characters he's talking about, or rather, we're not clear. It's a bit ambiguous. At first they seem to have a self-restraint that he approves of but then he says "are themselves as stone" which sounds cold and unfeeling, and as it goes on this – er – ambiguity is continued in words like "rightly" in "they rightly do inherit"...'

There was a knock at the door. Relieved, Martin called 'Yes' and a girl entered, breathless, asking, 'Is this Martin Philpot's criticism group?'

Martin gave a broad smile.

'Miss Kirkham, we presume. We thought we had lost you to the social scientists, did we not? You are very late.'

'I'm terribly sorry. Actually I did get lost. I was in the wrong building. I think it must have been biology or something. There were glass tanks with rats and goldfish everywhere and I asked someone and they'd never heard of you and I knew I must be in the wrong place because everyone in the English department has heard of you. I'm awfully sorry.'

Martin longed to ask the causes of his fame but his fear of revealing his vanity was stronger than his vanity.

'Well we're glad you found us at last. By some freak of injustice, the last to arrive gets the comfortable chair so sit down and read this.'

'Oh thank you. How kind of you.'

'Not at all. Part of the day's work. Let me introduce Mr. Hamilton, Mr O'Reilly, Miss Martin, Mr.. er.. Sellingwood-, no, Sillington-Kirby. We hope you'll be happy here.'

Miss Kirkham took off her coat which was a purer version of Sillington-Kirby's. Susan Martin's nostrils dilated imperceptibly as she seemed to be guessing whether the strong scent now wafting towards her was one that she recognised. It was apparent to all that under Miss Kirkham's thin ribbed sweater she wore no bra. Her bosom rose and fell as she recovered her breath. Martin caught O'Reilly gaping at her but was not confident that this had put him off his stride. He had been doing too well.

'Mr O'Reilly was telling us quite simply and very adequately what the poem is about. I think we'll give someone else a chance. Mr Hamilton.'

'I agree that it's diff... difff... difficult. But at the end of it all he doesn't like them. He calls them "lilies that f... fffff... ffff... fester".'

So the boy had a stutter. He didn't think the Irish ever had any difficulty in speaking.

'Why does he call them "lilies that fester"?'

'Because...'

'No. Mr O'Reilly. Let Mr Hamilton continue.'

'Lilies are like pure and untouchable, and unc... c... cor... corrupt and so when they, when they...'

Sillington-Kirby interrupted.

'I think it's obvious to anybody not blinkered with false

ideology that this poem is the product of a diseased consciousness. Why do we have to waste our time with such bourgeois crap?'

A tremor went around the room. Martin spoke as evenly as his delight would allow.

'Perhaps you would be good enough to explain what you mean by hm… bourgeois crap, Mr Sillington-Kirby?'

'Oh you know all this Desert Island Discs stuff, the Bible and Shakespeare. It's so fucking cosy! They're burning babies in Vietnam and here we are reading poems about lilies that fester. This whole fucking university festers if you ask me.'

'And what do you think we should read if we are to help the babies in Vietnam, may I ask?'

'Well not this crap for a start. It's totally irrelevant. It belongs to a parasitic culture that has outlived its usefulness.'

'I suppose you would prefer us to study the works of Mr Bob Dylan.'

'Oh *really*! No-one listens to *Dylan* any more!'

'Well poor Bob Dylan. Cast into the dustbin of history along with Shakespeare, Milton and Wordsworth I suppose. Perhaps you are aware of the fact that Karl Marx was a great admirer of Shakespeare, quoted him, knew hundreds of his lines by heart. Or is Marx a little passé himself these days?'

Sillington-Kirby made a sound indicative of withering

scorn but containing no words. Martin, beginning to enjoy himself, was now fully in control.

'Did anybody else know by the way that Marx admired Shakespeare?'

They all shook their heads except O'Reilly who nodded, a little reluctantly. Martin was surprised to see him flushed and giving every indication of discomfort. Susan Martin was staring hard at her piece of paper.

'Now that our "Sime" has aired his ignorance I think we'll return to the poem. Miss Martin you haven't said anything. Do you think this poem is… the product of a diseased consciousness?'

Miss Martin smiled. 'Well, no, but I do think he sounds rather bitter.'

'Yes. Interesting. Why bitter?'

'I don't know, that's just the feeling it gives me.'

'Oh dear. A creature of sensibility. Well I'm afraid that's not quite enough. Look at the poem and find words which display this bitterness you have remarked on.'

There was a silence. O'Reilly took a tin from his pocket and started to roll a cigarette. When it was finished he offered it to Michael who shook his head. Miss Kirkham added a further contribution to the fragrance of the room by lighting a *disque bleu*. Martin was suddenly reminded of her interview and how

212

she had told him that she had worked in France. She had chattered enthusiastically about Francoise Sagan.

'Miss Kirkham. I lust after your… cigarettes.' He took one from the packet on her knee. 'Thank you. *Droit de seigneur,*' he added leering slightly. She gave a gracious nod, but did not smile. 'Mr. O'Reilly, perhaps when you have finished contributing to the unemployment problems of the country… You look puzzled. Does it never occur to you that if everybody rolled their own cigarettes there would be cigarette factories closing down all over the country. Never mind. I jest. I jest, wearily, but I jest. Continue your exposition of the poem.'

'Well I'm beginning more and more to like the idea of people who have the power to hurt other people but who restrain themselves from doing so, but still. Shakespeare I think doesn't like these particular ones. I agree with… Mr. Hamilton. Eh that sounds daft. What's your name?'

'Michael.'

'Right. I agree with Mike. I think he ends up on a note of disgust about these people. And Susan's right too. It is bitter. These are aristocratic types he's talking about – that word "power" is important in the first line. Very important. You hold it in suspense in your mind and then you come to "lords and owners" "stewards" etc. You see how it fits in with the rest.

213

There's a hierarchy here, a class structure not only in the world of men but in nature too with the distinction between the weeds and flowers. And in the end, it gets reversed. The ruling class once they become corrupted are stinking worse than weeds. He's also emotionally involved...'

'Thank you Mr. O'Reilly. Are you a Marxist?'

Michael Hamilton flinched but O'Reilly seemed unperturbed.

'Yes.'

'Well, well what a lot of comrades we have here today. Miss Kirkham what have you to say about the poem. Is it to be the Moscow line or the line from Peking?'

'I don't know a thing about politics but I thought what he – indicating O'Reilly – said sounded perfectly all right. The only thing I'd also say is that it's obvious he's suffered some kind of emotional disappointment from one of these aristocratic blokes, I mean young men. The reason I say "young men" is that he was homosexual, wasn't he, and I expect he was doubly vulnerable I mean as a poet in a world of noblemen and also because he was susceptible to...'

'Miss Kirkham, Miss Kirkham. I wonder if you even aware that you are committing a heresy! You must be very wary indeed of the snares of the intentionalist fallacy. Nothing about Shakespeare's sexual proclivities is of the slightest relevance to our discussion. A poem is not to be read side by side with the biography of the poet – even if the biographer is Mr. Burgess. We must treat the poem as an aesthetic monad, Miss Kirkham. It is complete in itself. We must see the writer as non-intrusive, like the god of creation, and I am quoting James Joyce – removed, apart, indifferent, paring his fingernails – so let us not hear any gossip about fair youths or dark ladies. Let us return to the words on the page. You wanted to speak Mr. Sillington-Kirby.'

'I think what you're saying is probably just petit-bougeois escapism, but to get back to the poem, I now realise that it's about the corruption of the legal system in Shakespeare's time and so of course it is relevant because in our society the legal system is corrupt through and through like the police, the army, the education system…'

As Mr. Sillington-Kirby warmed to his subject, the group seemed to relax, only Mr. O'Reilly continuing to look embarrassed. Gradually the room filled with smoke. Once Martin got up to answer the telephone, once to open a window. Shortly after five o'clock he looked at his watch and said, 'Well, I think we'll call it a day. For next time I want one of you to choose a poem.' They all looked hard at the table. 'Miss Kirkham, how about you? Any poet you like, but not, I beg you, Dylan Thomas unless you really must. Everybody chooses

Dylan Thomas. Come and see me when you've decided and I'll get copies made. All right. Off you go.'

They filed out. Sillington-Kirby rushed towards the lift as if a telegram had summoned him to momentous events. The girls went through a door marked WOMEN. In front of the mirror, Catherine Kirkham scowled and started pulling and tweaking savagely at her streaked hair in order to dishevel it. Susan's face retained its sweetness of expression as she too ruffled her hair, but more gently. (She looked as if she had just got out of bed but could be persuaded to get back in again was the effect she was after.)

'What a horrible little creep!' exclaimed Catherine.

Susan started. 'Who?'

'Him. Philpot of course.'

'You could hardly call him little.' Susan leaned forward to smudge her eyeliner a little, 'I think I quite liked him.'

'*Liked* him? But he's perfectly horrible. So pompous. Why did he have to put everyone down all the time?'

'I expect that's just his manner. He's probably very shy underneath.'

Meanwhile on the way to the lift, O'Reilly said to Michael, 'If you're Michael Hamilton there's a parcel for you at the porter's desk. My name's Dave, by the way.'

'Pleased to meet you Dave. Is that the porter's desk in

the main building?'

'Yes I'm going that way if you're walking over now.'

'Well what did you make of that lot?' he ventured.

'What the group?'

'Well you know, the whole thing I meant really'

'Desperate. Seems a real weirdo, doesn't he, Philpot? See the way he asked you if you were a Marxist. At my interview he asked straight out was I a Catholic. Jesus!'

'I wouldn't worry. He's just a liberal academic – none of it matters to him. He's probably not a bad bloke personally. He's shit scared of us.'

'What him? Scared of us?'

'He must be, why else do you think he talks like that? "Indeed Mr. Hamilton, that is most illuminating". I very much doubt if he talks to his wife like that.'

'I never thought of that. I thought they all talked that way.'

'What about Winterman then?'

'Who's he?'

'You know Arnold Winterman. Introduction to the Novel this morning. Bloke with a Cockney accent.'

'Was there a lecture this morning?'

'Yes didn't you get a timetable?'

'I did but I couldn't make any sense of it. I thought

lectures didn't start till the eleventh.'

'It's the eleventh today.'

'Is it? Fuck. I'll have to get organised all right.'

'You'd best get some nice fella like me to help you go over the time-table in that case.'

'Would you Dave? That'd be great. Did I miss much in the lecture?'

'Not really. It was all about Experiments in Form and Alternative Endings. He was on about some novel with two endings called The French Left and its Women. Did you ever read it?'

'No, sounds a funny kind of book to me.'

They headed across the campus, walking on a paved path already sinking into the muddy field. To the right was an unfinished building where bright yellow vehicles churned up more mud. The building they were approaching had been finished for some years but was surrounded by scaffolding on which were hung notices saying, DANGER FALLING TILES. 'If you want my view of a real weirdo, what about Sillington-Kirby?' said Dave.

Michael laughed, 'That guy's really crazy. I was relieved, mind, when he started talking, he took the pressure off me.'

'Did he? Well you didn't need him, you were doing

okay. That type really gets up my nose. Instant revolutionaries I call them. It would put anyone off socialism for life, like, listening to the kind of muck he was coming out with. Actually I think he's with the L.I.S.'

'What's that?'

'League for International Socialism. Lizzies we call them, or Lice depending how you feel about them. Crowd of morons if you ask me.'

They walked on in silence. The seminar had been an ordeal for Michael, not only because of the stammer, but because poetry had always been something he thought he understood. Often it had played a consoling role in his life. But suddenly today a poem had become a hostile thing to be grappled with. And now Dave was depressing him. He had liked him at once and had been cheered to talk to him. But how did he come to know so much? Not only could he understand the poem and talk about it articulately, but he could read the timetable, find his way around, knew about the L.I.S. whoever they were. It couldn't only be that he was English. Was the L.I.S. one of the groups they talked about in the Gweedore Bar? At the thought of the Gweedore he was filled with a homesick longing to be there. He tormented himself thinking of it as it might be on a Saturday night, crowded, the telly blathering away in the corner everyone ignoring it except when the match was on. A big pint set up in front of him, Gerry Lynch and Joe there maybe, and Julie...

'Are you thinking maybe I'm too hard about them Mike?'

'I was thinking this place is very cold. All those white buildings and this fucking great bleak field.'

'You're dead right. It's like science-fiction. You expect to hear Dr Who music any second.'

After a few minutes he added, 'Are you doing anything later on, because I was thinking we could go over the timetable and have a couple of pints if you can stand that apology for a shebeen they call the students' bar.'

'Good idea, Dave, sound. Very sound.'

'We could meet up in my room. I'm in E block. E244.'

'What time?'

'Whenever you like.'

'Thanks a lot mucker.'

They parted and Michael made his way towards the porter's desk, then turned, 'Hey Dave!'

'What number did you say your room was?'

From his window in the tower Martin watched them make their way across the muddy campus. He envied them their youth and sincerity and even their awkwardness. Would it be easier to breathe in a life unprotected by irony? He watched them separate, then come almost together again before finally heading in different directions.   What had they been saying? Something disparaging about the university, perhaps, about him? Then he thought, and it gave him pleasure to imagine it, maybe they were just saying 'See you tomorrow!'